M<

A Killer Coffee Mystery

Book Two

BY
TONYA KAPPES

Mocha and Murder

Fred's dairy farm was behind the house. I'd yet to get a tour, but I really wanted one. I'd also been using his heavy cream in most of my baking and cooking. Getting the real deal sometimes just made a recipe.

I reached in my car and grabbed my money along with the apple crisp cookies.

"Let's go find them," I said to Pepper. "Please God, don't let them have killed one another."

The shop door was open, so I walked right on in. Pepper went ahead of me and took liberty to smell all the new fun smells a working farm had to offer.

"Fred! Louise!" I called hoping they were in here.

When I didn't see anyone, I turned to head back outside.

Pepper had gone back outside. His bark alarmed me because he rarely barked. I ran out hoping he'd not gotten into it with a cow or bull. A big veterinarian bill wouldn't be at the top of my list if I could help it.

"Pepper, come," I called right before he took off into the apple orchard. "Pepper, no!"

Pepper kept on going. I ran after him and stopped at the second row of trees. Down the row a little I saw Louise. She was as still as a statue.

"Whoohooo! Louise," I hollered relieved to have found her. She didn't turn around so I started to walk down the row when I noticed she was standing over something. "Louise?" I asked getting a little closer. "Is everything okay?"

She turned around, clearing my line of vision.

"Does it look like it's okay?" she asked, a bloody knife in her hand with drops of blood dripping on the dead body of Fred Hill.

TONYA KAPPES
WEEKLY NEWSLETTER

Want a behind-the-scenes journey of me as a writer?
The ups and downs, new deals, book sales, giveaways and more? I share it all!

As a special thank you for joining, you'll get an exclusive copy of my cross-over short story, *A CHARMING BLEND.* Go to Tonyakappes.com and click on subscribe in the upper right corner to join.

CHAPTER ONE

"Good morning, Roxy," Low-retta Bebe eyed the apple honey crisps. Really her name was Loretta, but with her deep southern accent she pronounced it Low-retta. She played with a piece of her short black hair, tilted her head to the left and to the right.

"Good morning," I said with a plate of honey glazed donuts in one hand and a pot of coffee in the other.

The Bean Hive was booming for a Monday morning and I was never so thankful when I saw Bunny Bowowski coming through the door on my way over to the customers.

"Here are your donuts and hot coffee." I set the plate down. I ran my hand down my apron. "Give me a holler if you need anything else."

The customers nodded.

"It's a busy morning. I told you I can come in early," Bunny said as she grabbed an apron off the coat rack that stood next to the counter.

"I'm so grateful you are here, but I can't be wearing out my best employee." I winked.

"I'm your only employee and I think I get around good for an old broad." She tucked a piece of her grey, chin-length hair behind her ear.

She let out a puff of air, her bangs flew up in the air. "Now, what does Loretta want?"

I leaned into Bunny. "I'm not sure. She's been eyeing the crisps for a while." I straightened back up. "Do you mind going into the kitchen and grabbing some of the macaroons out of the freezer? It looks like we are having a macaroon kind of day."

"Hey, Low-retta, been to the tanning bed lately?" Bunny snickered before she hurried back to the kitchen.

"Well, I never," Loretta scoffed, though she couldn't deny that the tan she had didn't come from any sort of natural sun. The woman was brown all year around. She claimed she was Cherokee, which she might've been, but the lines in her neck when she lifted her chin showed an all-together different shade of skin that told me she was ninety percent tanning bed.

"Oh, you know Bunny." I tried to cover up Bunny's lack of self-discipline when it came to her mouth. Bunny was in her seventies and she didn't have any sort of filter. It was as if there was an age where the filter of the mouth seems to disappear and that age seemed to be around the seventy marker. "She's just jealous she can't look as good as you."

"Are you saying I'm an old bat like her?" Loretta's eyes narrowed, her chin lifted and she looked down her nose at me.

"Absolutely not. I'm saying that not many people can look as nice as you." Again, I had to grit my teeth to keep my eyes from rolling.

"Hmm." Loretta ho-hummed and turned back to the glass counter to look at the apple honey crisps.

All the café tables were filled and the stools that butted up to the window counter at the front of the coffeehouse were also occupied. Most of them had totes that were overflowing with beach towels. The Bean Hive was located in the middle of the boardwalk and had the best view of the lake. The sun was out and the day looked like it was going to cooperate with all the boaters. The lake was calm and the boardwalk was full with people. It was going to be a great summer.

Before I headed back to the counter I checked the coffee and tea stations, both at opposite ends of the coffeehouse, to make sure the creamers were still fresh and the coffee pots were hot and steaming like my customers liked it. The coffee bar had six industrial thermoses that included different blends as well as decaffeinated. The tea bar had a nice selection of different loose-leaf teas for hot or cold drinks. Plus a wide variety of gourmet teas were there to choose from along with a choice of antique teapots I'd gotten from Wild and Whimsy Antiques which was located on the end of the boardwalk.

I'd opted to hang large chalkboards above the L-shaped glass countertop. The first chalkboard hung over the pies and cookies. It listed the weekly selections along with prices. The tortes and quiches were in the middle glass counter and the chalkboard hung overtop. The third chalkboard hung above the counter before the bend in the L and listed the weekly casseroles along with the specialty drinks. The chalkboard on the small side of the L-shaped counter had information about catering along with some lunch options that sometimes included soups.

Loretta looked as if she were reading every single word on each chalkboard.

Summers in Honey Springs, Kentucky always brought in a good amount of tourists but the renovation of the boardwalk and the arrival of summer really brought in the outsiders.

"How's it going?" I asked Loretta on my way back to the counter.

"Well," she let out a long sigh, "the Southern Women's Club is having our last meeting for the summer vacation." She pulled her hand up to the pearl necklace around her neck and ran the pad of her finger across them. "You know we convene for the summer." She said it like they were the United States Congress.

It took everything in my soul not to roll my eyes. When I moved to Honey Springs and opened The Bean Hive coffeehouse, I wanted to make sure I was part of the community, and joining Southern Women's Club was on my list. Loretta quickly let me know that I'd not proven myself to be in such a prestigious club. Yes, she was one of those southern women.

"I'm not sure if these will do. I mean." Her eyes drew up to mine when she realized she'd probably just insulted me.

"Here." I grabbed a white milk glass plate from one of the open shelves and slid open the door of the glass display case. "Why don't you try one and let you know what you think."

I handed her the plate of crisps with the brown and crispy outside, gooey in the middle and knew that when she took her first bite, the cinnamon, apple, and pastry mixture would melt her heart.

"You know, I try to use ingredients that are local. The honey glaze on top is from one of the bee farms and the apples are from Hill's Orchard." I was proud that I could support and buy from local vendors.

As soon as she lifted the pastry to her lips and took a bite, her shoulders relaxed, her eyes closed and she chewed with a delightful glow on her tanned face.

"Oh my." A sigh escaped Loretta's lips. "These will do just fine," she said. "Is there oatmeal in there?"

Did Loretta smile? The woman never smiled. The edges of her lips tipped up just enough that I was going to call it a smile.

"Yes, ma'am, there is." My heart soared. This was exactly why I enjoyed having a coffeehouse so much more than being a lawyer. The joys of seeing someone enjoy a fresh cup of coffee or a simple pastry was a way better feeling than telling a client that they were probably going to jail for life.

"I'll take three dozen by Thursday." She put the plate on the counter and clasped her hands.

"Thursday?" I questioned as my mind flipped through the days. Monday, Tuesday, Wednesday, I counted on my fingers and that included today.

"Is there a problem?" she asked snidely.

"Not at all." I questioned exactly what I'd just agreed to. "I'm doing the apples in my head. A baking thing." I lied knowing that Friday was the first day of the summer season and I still had to create something spectacular for the coffeehouse.

"I don't really care about all that." She waved her hand toward me. The sunlight dripping through the front windows of the shop caught the big diamond on her finger and made those little rainbow spots all over the coffeehouse. "As long as they are ready by Thursday."

Pepper jumped up from his dog bed and bounced around the coffeehouse trying to grab the rainbow spots.

"That's what you get when you get a pound dog." Loretta's brows arched. "Thursday." She turned on her heels and walked out of the coffeehouse.

"You're such a good boy," I called to Pepper, my salt and pepper Schnauzer, as he bounded toward me.

I grabbed one of the homemade dog treats I'd made fresh yesterday from the animal treat jar and tossed it to him. Happily, he munched on it.

The rest of the morning, Bunny and I spent a lot of time grabbing more pastries from the freezer. Today I was very thankful that I was closed a half day on Sundays so I could bake and freeze for busy days like these. Once the coffeehouse only had a couple of customers, I took the opportunity to take Pepper out for a quick walk on the boardwalk.

Quick was probably not the right word, because everyone loved my salt and pepper four-legged friend. He was friendly to everyone. Loretta was right. I'd moved to Honey Springs and purchased a small cabin that was a seven-minute bike ride to the boardwalk. It was great exercise for me, not to mention it helped wake me up for my four-thirty a.m. start time. Pepper didn't seem to mind riding in the bike basket.

The buzz of the boats coming in and out of the no-wake zone was a happy memory of the summers I'd spent in Honey Springs with my aunt Maxi. She was the reason my father would bring me here for summer vacations. He'd stay for a week and I'd stay for the summer.

The boardwalk didn't have as many stores back then, especially not a coffeehouse, but Crooked Cat bookstore had been there forever.

"Hey there, Roxy." Leslie Roarke, the owner of Crooked Cat, waved at me when she looked up after Pepper and I walked through the store's door. Her long, copper, kinky hair stuck up all over the place. I knew her pain. My hair was also very curly, but hers was worse than mine. "Pepper, you want a treat?" she called from the counter.

Treat was all Pepper needed to hear before he darted out in her direction.

"I got a new collection of books over there." She pointed to the new arrival shelf. "Anything in particular you're looking for?"

"I'm thinking about buying a bridal book." I lifted my hand in the air.

Recently I'd gotten engaged to my Honey Springs summer boyfriend, Patrick Cane. Of course we weren't teenagers anymore and some of the residents of Honey Springs think we are rushing into things, but it's not like I'm walking down the aisle tomorrow or even next month. In fact, Patrick and I hadn't even discussed a date.

"I don't think I have any, but there is one I can order that I think you'd like." Leslie had taken over Crooked Cat after her mother, Alexis, had been murdered. Not only was it a blow to her, but to the community. Alexis and Crooked Cat were staples in Honey Springs. I was just glad that Leslie had decided to stay.

"That'd be great." I offered a smile. It wasn't like Leslie and I were good friends. She actually didn't like Pepper the first time I'd met her. "I'm so glad you stayed in Honey Springs."

"Me too." She ran her hand down the store's cat that was curled up next to the register. "My mom would've loved this. It's a shame that I didn't take more time coming home."

"I'm sure your mother knows exactly what you're doing." It was only words, but I hoped they offered her some comfort. "You're keeping her hard work and memory alive."

"Thank you, Roxy. I really appreciate that." There was a tear in her eye. "I do love Honey Springs."

"Me and Crissy are going to meet at the coffeehouse around six for a quick supper before I have to go to Pet Palace if you'd like to join us." Crissy was going to kill me, but I thought Leslie needed friends.

"I'd love to." She grabbed a piece of paper. "I'm going to get right on ordering your book for you. My treat as an engagement present."

"That's so nice." I patted my leg. "Let's go Pepper. We've got to get back to the shop before Bunny gets too busy."

CHAPTER TWO

*B*unny and Louise Carlton were standing over the stove in the kitchen of the coffeehouse looking into a pot.

"What are y'all doing?" I asked and tied the apron around my waist.

"Thank gawd, you're back." Louise held a small dog in her arms and put it on the ground.

Immediately, Pepper rushed over to the poor shaking fur ball to check it out. All of us stood there waiting to see if we needed to step in. Pepper wasn't going to hurt the little dog, but we didn't know how the introduction was going to work.

A sigh of relief escaped us when the little dog started to bounce around Pepper in a playful manner.

"I'm so glad she fits in." Louise's eyes dipped. Her jaw relaxed. "Now, can you make me a chai? Bunny and I can't figure it out for nothing."

Bunny walked back into the coffeehouse to take care of any customers while I made Louise's custom chai tea.

"Tell me about the dog." I turned the gas knob on the stove to high to bring the water to a boil.

"Tank came from a fraternity boy." She rolled her eyes and eased herself down on one of the stools that were next to the kitchen island where I prepared most of the foods. "I don't know why these college kids think they can take care of a dog when they can barely take care of or feed themselves."

"I'm glad he brought Tank to you." I retrieved the cardamom, cinnamon powder, star anise, fennel seed, nutmeg, ginger, cloves and peppercorn that I used to make her tea. "Without Pet Palace I'm not sure what the animals in Honey Springs would do."

Pet Palace was Honey Springs's take on a local SPCA. Not all small towns in Kentucky had an animal shelter and Pet Palace was solely run on volunteers and donated money. Louise never turned away an animal of any kind. Every Monday night I volunteered to clean cages and feed the animals.

"Without you, they'd never get the exposure they needed to find a good home." She leaned in on the counter, propping her elbows up and resting her chin in her hands.

"I love having them here." I stirred in the ingredients as the water boiled. "Unfortunately I can't contribute with money, but I can offer my coffeehouse and time."

The coffeehouse was a dream for me. I'd become a lawyer like my own mother had dreamed. Married another law student and we opened our own practice. After I'd caught him taking more than a monetary payment from one of our clients, we'd gotten divorced. Aunt Maxi had asked me to come visit like I did when I was a child. Then she told me about the plans to revitalize the boardwalk and subtly she planted the seed that I should move there and she'd let me put my own coffeehouse in one of the two buildings she owned on the boardwalk: Crooked Cat, which I'd never allow her to kick out, and the building where the coffeehouse sat today.

Without much thinking, I drained my bank account to open the coffeehouse and buy the cabin; I was now a part of the Honey Springs community. My way of giving back to such a wonderful cause as Pet Palace, I came up with the idea that one animal a week could be featured at the coffeehouse since we had a lot of traffic. They could live in the coffeehouse during the week. Luckily, there hadn't been any backlash from the community and the local health department kept a close eye on me to make sure they didn't enter the kitchen. Our success rate was one hundred percent and most of the time the animals were adopted within the first forty-eight hours of coming to the coffeehouse.

"I put all his paperwork and information in a red folder underneath your counter out there." She pointed and grabbed an apple out of the basket. "You've already been to the Farmer's Market today?"

I grabbed a teacup off the rack and carefully poured Louise's tea. I set it in front of her and moseyed over to the refrigerator to get her creamer.

"No, in fact I've got to get over there and call Patrick to take me." I dragged my phone out and quickly texted him. "Loretta Bebe came in and actually asked me to make some apple honey crisps for the last meeting of the year for the Southern Women's Club. Can you believe it?"

"Low-retta is a pushover. She just acts like she's mightier than thou. Plus, you and all your goodies are the talk of Honey Springs. She knows that she needs to hire you before you get too busy. She'll brag on how she discovered you." Louise rolled her eyes so big it was enough for the both of us. "Do you mind putting this into a to-go cup? I've got a full day."

"Sure." I didn't hesitate. I had a full day too and getting to the Farmer's Market to get the best apples Mr. Hill had was my number one priority.

CHAPTER THREE

"You didn't have to take off work to bring me to the Farmer's Market." I said to Patrick, though I was so glad he did because the market was already packed. "But I really appreciate it. I could've biked, but with all the apples I need or if I'd planned better, I could've driven my car today to the coffeehouse."

"What's the benefit of running a company if I can't take off a few hours? Besides, Steve has got it under control." He referred to Steve Arpel, one of his employees.

I looked over at Patrick. His chiseled jaw tensed. His hand twisted around his dog's leash, pulling Sassy closer to him. Pepper and Tank followed her as if I too had tugged on their leashes, though I hadn't.

Sassy was a black standard poodle that Patrick had adopted and she certainly lived up to her name. She was a sassy dog that barely gave anyone but him and Pepper the time of day.

When I looked at Patrick, I saw past the few wrinkles that'd made a home around his eyes and the touches of grey that dotted his brown crew cut and saw the tender smile and loving brown eyes that I'd fallen head over heels in love with as a teenage girl. He might've aged on the outside like me, but his heart and depths of his eyes told me his true soul.

The first day he walked into The Bean Hive, he walked right back into my heart.

Whoever passed us took a moment to pet the dogs. How could they not when Pepper rubbed up against any human leg that walked past him. Tank wasn't a bit timid when it came to being pet. Whoever pet him, I handed a Pet Palace card and gave a brief story on how to adopt Tank.

"Steve's a quick learner." It was nice how Steve was able to just pick up where Patrick needed him. It was hard to find an employee like that. "That must feel good."

The Farmer's Market was every Monday downtown in Central Park. It was a five-minute drive from the boardwalk but I liked to bike there. Especially since the weather had really turned. Just a week ago the morning still held the crisp cool air that was left over from winter that required a jacket or cozy sweatshirt. Today the temperature started out in the mid-sixties and was only going up from there.

"Very good. It sure is a nice day to be playing hooky." Patrick winked and held my hand as we walked across the street to Central Park. The dogs trailing next to us. "And playing it with you."

Sassy nudged between us. Tank yipped at her. We laughed.

"You too, girl." He let go of my hand and patted her curly hair. "We are going to find you a perfect home." He picked up Tank. His head darted around as Tank tried to lick all over his face.

The park was smack dab in the middle of town with a sidewalk around the perimeter. There was a gazebo in the middle and on any given warm summer day, many people sat there and read or even enjoyed their lunch.

The summertime Honey Springs flags with a scene of the lake and boardwalk flapped in the light breeze as they hung from the dowel rods on the carriage lights that dotted the downtown sidewalks. The wild-flowers made a colorful landscape around the park with the vibrant purple, pink, yellow, white, and blue colors. This was just the beginning of the beauty Mother Nature drew in our cozy town.

The courthouse, medical building, the library along with a few specialty shops were located in the middle of Main Street across from the park.

"So what is going on with you?" Patrick stopped right in front of Honey Bee Company's booth at the Farmer's Market. He hooked the handle of Sassy's leash around his wrist. He set Tank back on the ground.

I took Tank's leash and attached it to my wrist to free up my hand.

Honey Bee Company had the best tasting honey that went perfectly with most of my specialty teas. They also kept the comb in the honey jar, which was best for baking.

"I don't know." I shrugged and picked up a jar so I didn't have to look at Patrick.

He reached down and took the jar from my hands, forcing me to look up at him.

"You can tell me." There was a deep concern in his eyes. "I can tell there's something on your mind."

I handed the sales lady a five-dollar bill and put the jar of honey in the grocery bag I'd brought with me. The cotton bag swung back and forth as we walked to Hill's Orchard fruit stand, owned by Fred Hill. He had the perfect apples for my apple tart. This time of the year was hard to find that perfect apple that had the sweet and tart, but somehow Fred never disappointed.

"I've been thinking." I grabbed his hand to stop in front of the apples at Mr. Hill's stand. "I know the teenage Patrick really well. I've only been back to Honey Springs for six months fulltime. I want to date you." I scanned the table lined with orchard baskets filled with all sorts of freshly picked apples. The stems and leaves were still on them.

"We have a lifetime of dating ahead of us." He brought my hand up to my own eyes to get a glimpse of my ring. "Or did you forget about this?" He kissed my ring before he dropped our hands back down.

"Of course I didn't forget that." I smiled. He did tug my heartstrings. I pulled my hand away and grabbed a few apples and put them in my bag.

There were a few more apples I wanted, so I'd get them and tally them up and pay when I was finished. Besides, Fred and his wife Jean were busy helping other customers. We'd made eye contact so he knew I was there for my weekly fruit.

"Are you saying you don't want to marry me?" Patrick's voice cracked.

"No, no." I shook my head. "It's been the best couple of months of my life." I put my hand on my heart. "You are amazing. I don't want to get another divorce and I worry about how well we know each other."

"We love each other, isn't that enough?" he asked.

"Patrick." My head tilted to the side. The sun grazed my shoulder and gave a spotlight on his face. There was a hurt in his eyes that made my heart break. "Do you even know my favorite movie? My favorite food? Color?"

"No. But I know what's in there." He pointed to my heart.

"Yes you do. There's no harm in taking the time to go on a few dates, get to really know each other." It made perfect sense to me and sounded like a good plan. "We aren't going anywhere. It isn't like we have a date to get married, just taking some time to really get to know each other."

He dragged his hand up and scratched his head.

"If that's what you want." He blinked a few times. There was a thin smile on his lips as he spoke. "I'll do whatever needs to be done. I love you."

"I love you too." I curled up on my toes and gave him a kiss. "It'll be fun," my voice escalated in an excited tone. Now I felt like a heel. I probably should've just made dates and not told him my underlying meaning. "You love to fish. So take me fishing. Let me love it."

"I don't expect you to love my hobbies. Just like I don't love to bake or love coffee like you." He had a point.

My body slumped. I looked at him and let out a long sigh. Out of the corner of my eye, I could see and hear Louise Carlton having a heated conversation with Fred. She leaned way over an apple basket shaking a finger at him. Both of them fussing at the same time. Who knew how they could hear each other.

"Fine." He curled me into his big arms and kissed the top of my head. I could almost feel his thoughts. He was worried, but he'd see that there was no reason to be and my suggestion would make us stronger. "We will only grow stronger."

I wanted to believe his words, but the look on his face was as if I'd taken out his heart and stomped my cowboy boots on it over and over again until it was as thin as a cake of soap.

"That's right." I looked up, and with a soft sigh, he gently kissed me.

The loud bickering made me pull away.

"What's going on with Louise? She looks mad," Patrick said.

"I don't know." I tugged on Pepper's leash for him to stop sniffing and to follow me over to her. Patrick and Sassy followed me.

"That was not what we agreed to and I'm afraid I'm going to have to take Bertie back," Louise tried to modulate her voice as she fought to maintain control.

"That's not going to happen. I need Bertie to continue to lay the eggs that I need to keep my booth here at the Farmer's Market. If you dare step a foot on my property. . ." He curled his lips together.

"You'll what? Egg my car?" Louise's nostrils flared.

It was a side of Louise I'd never seen. She was always so kind and even-keeled.

"It's not a good day, Louise. I suggest you step away. I adopted Bertie fair and square." He shook his finger back at her. It was a finger shake off. "Don't make me call the police on you because you heard what Officer Shepard said last time I did."

"I don't care if they take away my license. I have to save Bertie," she spat through her gritted teeth. "I don't care what Spencer said either."

"Excuse me," I stepped in and smiled at both of them. "Pepper and Tank wanted to say hello."

Fred and Louise became silent but stared at each other. Pepper scurried over to get a good scratch.

"I've got to go." Louise jerked around. "Roxy, I'll talk to you later."

"Sure." I shrugged and looked at Fred. He didn't say anything. He went back to his produce.

"That was very odd." Patrick arched a sly brow.

"Very." I inhaled deeply and watched Louise run across the road, nearly missing getting hit by a car before she got into hers. "Very." I exhaled with a thankful sigh that she didn't get flattened.

CHAPTER FOUR

"*E*rrrt-uh-errr-uh-errrrrrrrr!" The sound of a chicken roused me from my deep sleep.

Pepper jumped up from the makeshift pallet I'd made for him on the floor of the Pet Palace office and barked loudly.

My head flew up in the air. My heart nearly pounded out of my chest. For one glorious minute, I'd fallen asleep and completely forgotten how tired I was since I'd been running around all day like a chicken with my head cut off.

A massive figure stood at the office door. Monday night was my volunteer night. Most Mondays I wasn't tired, I was plum wore out.

"Errrt-uh-errr-uh-errrrrrrrr!" The sound of the chicken came with the person at the door.

The man's shoulders filled his red and black checkered plaid coat. His fat face melted into a buttery smile. "You got a little drool." He motioned to his chin with the free hand that wasn't holding the feathered chicken. "I wasn't expecting to see you, Roxy."

I swiped the back of my hand across my face and patted down my hair because I knew it was sticking straight up. It would definitely be sprung up around my head since I'd been sleeping. My eyes adjusted. The figure sharpened.

"Mr. Hill." I greeted him when I realized who it was. "I'm sorry. You must be here to see Louise. She isn't here." I stood up, brushing my hands down the front of my shirt. I walked forward, stopping in front of him. "You can leave her a note if you want."

When I first volunteered to help out, I thought it'd be fun, but it was really hard work to clean all the kennels, feed, and play with the animals.

Mr. Hill stepped aside. He had on his John Deere green baseball cap pulled way down on his forehead. The bottom of his lip stuck out on the right where there was a big piece of chewing tobacco.

"Ah!" I jumped back when out of the corner of my eye I saw the bird's beak coming at me.

He laughed. "This here is Bertie." He referred to the feathery fowl.

"Errrt-uh-errr-uh-errrrrrrrr!" The big chicken crowed again. Pepper's nails ticked on the concrete floor as he did his little jig trying to get a good smell of Bertie.

"Hi, Bertie." I giggled. Never in a million years and certainly not this time a year ago did I ever think I'd be volunteering at a kennel and petting a chicken.

"You tell Louise that I stopped by." His face suddenly tensed. He pulled Bertie closer to his body. "You can also tell her to stay off my property or else."

I gulped.

His eyes lowered, as did his voice, "Are you still one of them lawyers?"

I nodded.

"Is everything okay in here?" Spencer Shepard asked when he appeared down the hall. "I saw some lights on while doing my nightly rounds and didn't realize anyone was here this late."

"Everything is just fine." Fred looked at Spencer. "I was just telling Roxy to leave Louise a message from me. Stay off my property." This time there was no doubt in my mind that Mr. Hill meant it.

"I'll be sure to tell Louise." I took Mr. Hill by the arm that wasn't carrying Bertie. I led him out of the office and to the front of Pet Palace where it was deserted.

There was a fireplace in the middle of the front room. The flame from the gas logs flickered giving the room a cozy feel and a few yips could be heard from the dog kennel side of the facility. Thanks to Patrick and Cane Contractors, Pet Palace had an all-new building and now they were working on the kennels. Soon the project would be complete and Louise would have the dream building she'd always imagined.

"How would you like it if someone harassed you all the time?" he asked as I unlocked the door.

"I wouldn't." I offered a smile and showed him out the door.

"What was that all about?" Spencer walked up behind me.

I locked the door.

"I have no idea." My hand lingered on the door handle as I wondered how on earth he'd gotten in there. "There's some bad blood between the two. I didn't get to ask her about it. In fact," I leaned up against the glass door and watched Mr. Hill's taillights until they disappeared into the dark night. "I had to break up an argument between them at the Farmer's Market."

He looked up at the ceiling and rolled those green eyes.

"So what are you doing here so late?" he asked.

"I fell asleep." I dragged my phone from my back pocket. It was close to eleven o'clock. Way past my bedtime. There were several missed calls from Patrick. I bet he was terrified where I was. I'd text him when I got home. "I've got to get home."

"Gather your things. I'm not letting you bike in the dark at this hour." He pointed to my bike that was leaning up against the outside of the building. "I'll take you and Pepper home."

Like good citizens, Pepper and I accepted his ride with my bike strapped into the open trunk of his sheriff's car. Pepper sat right up front and in the middle of us.

I needed air. I rolled down the window just enough for a fresh breath.

He stopped the cruiser at the stop sign in the middle of downtown near Central Park where the Farmer's Market was held. "Now what are you thinking about?"

My eyes raked over the park. The whole day had been strange beginning with the Farmer's Market scuffle between Louise and Mr. Hill.

"I was just thinking about Mr. Hill. He sure does have something to tell Louise. She sure did have a bone to pick with him," I said and shifted in my seat.

The streetlights along Main Street lit up the streets like it was daytime. The twinkling lights around the gazebo in the middle of Central Park looked like the fireflies that would soon be blanketing Honey Springs.

"The summer crowd is coming up, isn't it?" I decided to change the subject. I fiddled with the engagement ring.

The summer held fond memories from my teenage years. Patrick and I thought we were big shots hanging out by the lake, listening to the banjos and trying to catch fireflies.

"It sure is." Spencer continued to talk about how crowded the lake was going to be with boats and skiers.

I let out a few mmm-hmms, yeps, and un-huhs, but I wasn't listening to a word he said, and before I knew it, we were pulling up to my little cabin where Patrick was sitting on the front porch in a rocking chair along with . . .

"Mother?" My jaw dropped.

CHAPTER FIVE

"*R*oxy, we've been worried sick." Mom stood up.

It was like looking into a mirror. It was obvious whom I looked like.

"Patrick." Spencer nodded after Patrick stood up.

"Is something wrong?" Patrick asked and stood up. "Roxy, are you okay?"

"I'm fine." I opened the back door of the cruiser. Pepper jumped out and bounced toward the cabin. "I fell asleep at Pet Palace and Spencer was kind enough to give us a ride home."

Spencer had walked around to the back of the cruiser where he unhitched my bike. Patrick walked back to give him a hand and once it was free, Patrick walked it up to the porch.

"I was worried sick when you didn't answer your phone so I rushed over." He looked between my mother and me. "At first glance I thought it was you that was waiting on the porch."

"Surprise." Mom did spirit hands in front of her body. "I'm guessing I'm the last person you expected to see on your porch."

"Where are my manners?" I was so shocked to see my mom that my brain had melted into mush. "You obviously already know Patrick."

"Your fiancé." She gave a cross look at Spencer.

"This is Spencer Shepard, the sheriff in Honey Springs." I gestured between the two. "Spencer, this here is Penny Bloom, my mother."

The two exchanged pleasantries.

"Did you know your mom was coming?" Patrick asked.

"No clue." I let out an exhausted sigh and opened my door. Pepper bolted in and immediately curled up in his dog bed next to the wood fireplace.

The cabin was pretty much an open floor plan. The right side was a small kitchen with open shelving; the left side of the cabin was a family room with a couple of comfy couches, wood fireplace, and a small TV. The bedroom was in the room on the left side of the small hallway and a bathroom on the right. My laundry room was in a closet in the bathroom and the washer and dryer were the stackable kind. There was a loft upstairs that had a murphy bed, but I mainly used it for storage.

Over the past ten years of doing the adulthood thing, I'd accumulated some stuff that I wasn't prepared to get rid of. Mainly law books, some photos, and a few things from my childhood. All of which my mother didn't really participate in.

"Of all the people who would come to Honey Springs, I'd have never guessed you," I said when she walked into the cabin.

Not that I really minded my mother being there, it was that she didn't like Honey Springs. When I was a child and my dad would even start to talk about my annual summer trip, my mother would go off the rail on how Aunt Maxi was nothing but a loon and there was no sense in me staying with her. It was the only time I ever heard my parents fight. And it was always about Honey Springs.

"I thought you were off on some grand adventure with what's his name." I could feel my patience thinning with the unneeded stress that Mom seemed to bring on me.

"I was off on a grand adventure." She rocked back on her heels and kept an eye on me. "But I missed my daughter. I called you several times, which you didn't answer and so I had to resort to calling your aunt Maxi."

"Really?" I walked around the cabin and tidied up what was already tidy. It kept me busy. "Because she never said a word."

"Of course she didn't. She always wanted you for herself. She was the one that told me about you and my soon-to-be son-in-law." Her shoulders did a shimmy-shake. "I can't wait to go dress shopping with you for your dress and, of course, one for the mother of the bride."

"Whoa." I looked at the time. "We don't have a date set and no dress shopping. I'm going to bed. Four-thirty comes awfully early."

Patrick seemed to be taking it all in. He'd known about my mother and how we had a strained relationship. It wasn't like I didn't talk about her. I'm pretty sure every summer I cried leaving Honey Springs because I didn't want to go home. Not that my mother and I didn't get along, we did. We just didn't have that mother-daughter relationship that most of my friends had.

"I'm glad you're okay. And I can tell you've had your fill." Patrick eased the tension with a sweet kiss and a big bear hug. "We can talk in the morning."

His hand slid down my arm and clasped his fingers around mine. We walked outside and stood on the porch, looking out into the black night. The bullfrogs croaked in the distance, the crickets happily played their song and the hum of a fishing boat echoed from Lake Honey Springs.

"Are you going to be okay?" he asked.

"I'll be fine. I'll see you in the morning," I assured him.

When I went back inside, Mom must've been worn out. It looked like she'd sat down on the couch and went to rest her eyes, but passed out cold instead.

The next morning the alarm went off at the right time. Four-thirty a.m. Mom was fast asleep. She was a deep sleeper so I knew I could make a little noise and not wake her up. Pepper and I did our best to be quiet. There was no way I wanted to get into why she was really here. I mean really here. The bike ride to the coffeehouse was exactly the fresh breath I needed to get my morning started.

"I heard there was a scuffle down at the Farmer's Market yesterday,"

Bunny asked when we had a second to catch our breath after the lunch rush.

Tank and Pepper were snuggled up on Pepper's bed Patrick had gotten for him from Walk In The Bark Pet Boutique a few doors down. They'd been loved on so much from the crowd in the coffeehouse from breakfast to lunch, they were exhausted.

On most days, the lunchtime crowds stroll in for a dessert and coffee treat or they are on their lunch break and need a cake or some sort of sweet treat for their home. For those customers looking for more than to satisfy their sweet tooth, I make a couple baked casseroles or quiches each day.

Today was Kentucky hot brown day and by the time the lunch rush was over, there was only a four-inch square left of the fifteen hot browns I'd made.

"You did?" I scooped the leftover piece and put it on a plate, sliding it across the kitchen prep island for Bunny to enjoy.

I poured myself a cup of coffee. It'd been so busy this morning that I'd not been able to finish a cup and I needed it.

Pepper got out of his bed and walked over. His nose stuck up in the air curious to see if I was making him some treats. I'd already made a big batch over the weekend that would last the entire week of four-legged customers that came in with their two-legged owners. Every Sunday The Bean Hive was closed half of a day. I spent the closed time preparing all the baked goods for the week and that included the animal treats.

I flipped the lid on Pepper's jar of treats that sat on the counter and tossed him a special treat. He took it back to his bed and savored every morsel.

"I also heard you dissolved it." She licked her lips before she put a big forkful in her mouth.

"Oh no," I gasped and looked at the bag of apples that I'd completely forgotten to pay for. "I didn't pay Fred for my apples."

"Because you were talking Louise off her rocker?" She smiled knowing she'd had me and that I was about to spill my guts.

I dragged the bag over to the counter and lined up the granny smith apples. According to the clock, I could make and bake a few dozen of my delicious apple honey crisps. Fred Hill would have to forgive me and accept my apology along with my payment if I took him some crisp cookies made with his freshly picked apples.

"You've got a funny look in your eye," Bunny muttered with the last bite of the hot brown in her mouth.

"I'm going to take Fred Hill some of my apple honey crisps, pay for my apples, and then I'll tell you about the little mishap at the market," I chewed on my words but didn't delay.

The stems of the apples needed to be plucked and the apples needed to be cleaned and cut to make perfectly sized apple chunks.

"Do you think you can manage out front while I get to baking?" I asked and threw a clean apron over my head and tied it snuggly around my waist.

"Take your own sweet time." Bunny walked over to the dishwasher, putting her dish in. "I've got nothing to do but help you. I'll be sure to get Tank out for a walk too."

"You are the best, Bunny," I said.

I quickly cut and peeled five of the apples, tossed them in lemon juice and set them aside so I could get the rest of the ingredients ready and mixed. After I'd made the special oatmeal cookie cups and formed them in the cupcake pan, I filled each one with the apple filling, and stuck them in the oven.

Over the next thirty minutes I peeled, chopped, mixed and filled all the cupcake pans I had and stuck them on the baking rack in the refrigerator. There were a couple sugar cookies and mini blueberry muffins I pulled out to make room for all of the apple crisp pans. I stuck those in the oven and knew when I left to take Fred the treat and his money I'd be able to leave Bunny with enough stock to get her through until closing time.

The sweet and savory aroma of the apple crisp floated in the air, making my mouth water. The edges of the oatmeal cookie were golden brown and the center apple filling bubbled a little, a sure sign the cookie was cooked perfectly.

With the kitchen cleaned and the coffeehouse restocked for the rest of the day's customers, Pepper and I biked back to the cabin. Pepper was careful not to crush Mr. Hill's treat that was in the basket next to him.

"Mom," I called when I walked into the house to grab my car keys that were sitting in a basket on my kitchen counter.

When she didn't answer, I looked around, figuring she'd taken a walk to the lake. It was turning out to be a beautiful early summer day. Perfect weather for a nice walk or even a light hike along the shore.

"Ready, Pepper?" I didn't have to worry about grabbing a leash for Pepper. He was so good at commands and sticking close to my side. I was very fortunate.

Pepper's back legs were planted on the seat and his front paws were on the door handle with his nose pressed up against the glass. I hit the automatic window button. He stuck his head out and shook his head in the breeze as the wind whipped in his bushy grey brows and mustache. I never knew the joy a dog could bring until I'd gone to Pet Palace with Louise and he'd stolen my heart.

Thinking of Louise, I'd decided to give her a quick call and let her know I'd be there in an hour or so. Hopefully by the time I was done visiting with Fred, I'd have a few answers as to why she was so mad at him and be able to help her get over it when I went to see her.

"Call Pet Palace," I spoke to the built-in phone program in my car.

The phone rang and rang until the answering machine finally picked up. That struck me as strange. I'd never known her to leave the front desk un-manned. I left her a quick message reminding her of how I told her I was going to stop by.

Hill's Orchard, along with most of the farms, was on the complete opposite side of Honey Springs. The only way to get there was taking the old, curvy, uneven roads that could stand to have new pavement laid. Many of the farmers groaned how much this was needed at the council meetings and could use any extra money for the job, but the

Beautification Committee took the money with the council's approval and that's how the revitalization of the boardwalk happened. Without that, The Bean Hive would've never been a dream come true of mine.

In fact, Hill's Orchard wasn't too far from Pet Palace. It might be an early night, I happily sighed thinking I'd be able to stop by and pay Patrick a surprise visit. Since the nights were getting longer and the sun stayed out until around nine p.m., Pepper and I might get in a nice porch sitting night with him and Sassy.

I rolled down all the windows and let the air flow through the open car windows; the fresh air helped me clear out my head with how I'd hurt Patrick.

It wasn't like anything was going to change between us. We were going to date and do things that each other liked. Though I wasn't sure I'd get him on a bicycle.

The warm air flowed through the car. I flipped on the radio to listen to some great old country. Dolly Parton was belting out how much she loved you and I sang along. Pepper howled, his nose up in the air, his ears pinned back on his head from the wind. The sunlight danced along with the music through the spaces of the leaves as my car drove underneath the canopy where they lined both sides.

After the third hairpin curve, there was a fork in the road. I had to stop every single time to remember Fred's directions from the first time I had to come to the orchard. "At the fork in the road remember the tine is the right time." It made no sense what-so-ever, but made perfect sense at the same time. Tine meaning fork in the road and right was the direction.

I veered right and when I got to the old weathered barn wood sign that said Hill's Orchard in bright red letters, I turned in. Fred took really good care of his land. The apple trees were on the right, the grapevines were on the left as far as the eye could see. I'd not tried any but I'd heard that his wife made the best preserves in all of Kentucky. I'm sure I'd be able to incorporate them into an amazing donut. My mind went into that weird baking mode where it miraculously came up with different concoctions to bake and try. My mind and my car came to an abrupt stop when I saw Louise's car parked next to the small market building.

"What is she doing here?" I threw the car in park and jumped out, but not before Pepper leapt over me and beat me to the punch.

I grabbed my phone and quickly texted Patrick.

Me: *Beautiful day. Pepper and I are at the orchard. I thought we'd stop by after.*

Pepper looked at me.

"I know," I grumbled. "We were going to surprise him, but I'm feeling awfully bad about us not being able to talk about our situation."

Pepper pawed at me.

"Thanks, buddy." I ran my hand over his wiry hair. Patrick hadn't texted me back. "Let's go."

I opened the door. Pepper couldn't wait. He leapt across me and pranced around smelling anything he could. Though not too far from me.

The sun was beating down and the glare from the metal building made me see spots. I put my hand over my brow to get a look around and see if I saw Fred & Louise. Fred's farmhouse had a nice long porch on the front and his rockers were empty. They weren't there.

Fred's dairy farm was behind the house. I'd yet to get a tour, but I really wanted one. I'd also been using his heavy cream in most of my baking and cooking. Getting the real deal sometimes just made a recipe.

I reached in my car and grabbed my money along with the apple crisp cookies.

"Let's go find them," I said to Pepper. "Please God, don't let them have killed one another."

The shop door was open, so I walked right on in. Pepper went ahead of me and took liberty to smell all the new fun smells a working farm had to offer.

"Fred! Louise!" I called hoping they were in here.

When I didn't see anyone, I turned to head back outside.

Pepper had gone back outside. His bark alarmed me because he rarely barked. I ran out hoping he'd not gotten into it with a cow or bull. A big veterinarian bill wouldn't be at the top of my list if I could help it.

"Pepper, come," I called right before he took off into the apple orchard. "Pepper, no!"

Pepper kept on going. I ran after him and stopped at the second row of trees. Down the row a little I saw Louise. She was as still as a statue.

"Whoohooo! Louise," I hollered relieved to have found her. She didn't turn around so I started to walk down the row when I noticed she was standing over something. "Louise?" I asked getting a little closer. "Is everything okay?"

She turned around, clearing my line of vision.

"Does it look like it's okay?" she asked, a bloody knife in her hand with drops of blood dripping on the dead body of Fred Hill.

CHAPTER SIX

S pencer was standing over Mr. Hill's body, helping Doc Hafler get the body on the stretcher to take him to the morgue. Doc Hafler had been the town's physician as far back as I could remember. He treated me every summer for poison ivy. He was also the Honey Springs County Coroner.

"This orchard is closed down until further notice." Spencer did a come-here finger motion to another officer. "I need you to get a sign up on the entrance of the orchard saying it's closed until further notice."

The officer nodded and scurried off. Spencer's eyes caught mine.

Louise and I used one of the apple trees as a barrier between Mr. Hill's body and us. Spencer had asked us to step aside and not go anywhere because he wanted to talk to us. Pepper knew to stay close to me.

"What in the world is going on?" an older man asked with a toothpick stuck in his teeth. It bounced up and down when he talked. "Is that Fred?"

The man had on a pair of overalls and a John Deere cap propped on the top of his head with the bill deeply creased. He was a burly man that stood six foot two. He took the toothpick out of his mouth.

Pepper walked over to the man and smelled his shoes.

"It is." Louise rubbed the back of her neck. "I came out here and found him."

"You found him?" The man frowned.

"Yes," Louise whispered, barely audible over the squeak of the wheels of the stretcher.

"Who might you be?" the man asked me, wasting no time. He shuffled his shoe toward Pepper. I scowled.

"I'm Roxanne Bloom." I offered a thin smile. "That's my dog, Pepper."

"The coffee girl?" His brows drew together and looked down at Pepper. "I've heard about your shop. I'm not much of a fancy coffee drinker. I like mine black and simple."

"Just exactly how I like mine," I said. I patted my leg and Pepper came over. I gave him a good scratch on the side of his neck before he sat down at my feet. "You should come down and we'll have a cup together. On the house."

He stuck the toothpick back in his mouth. His eyes drew down to my hands where I was still carrying the apple crisps.

"I'm sorry. I didn't catch your name." I lifted my hands and peeled back the tin foil I'd pinched around the plate of the crisps, offering him and Louise one.

"I'm so sorry." Louise stopped her stare from watching Doc push the stretcher down the row of apple trees and to the ambulance. She shook her head. "Where are my manners? TJ Holmes, Roxy Bloom." She sucked in a deep breath. "TJ is Fred's neighbor."

TJ looked at my crisps. I lifted the plate toward him.

"Please, have some," I said. "These are from Fred's apples I bought at the Farmer's Market. I was bringing him some so he could taste how wonderful his apples truly are."

"You buy your fresh produce from him?" he asked and reached for one of the crisps.

"I do," I said and watched as TJ looked over the crisp.

Spencer glanced over at us, I caught his eye, giving him a nod. We'd been in this situation a few months ago when I found another body of a local woman.

He walked over to us with his notebook in his hand, a pen in the other. Pepper jumped to his feet. He really liked Spencer. Spencer squatted down, putting the pen and notebook in one hand and rubbed down Pepper's wiry silver fur with the other.

"Ladies, TJ," he greeted us with a low voice and stood back up.

"Sheriff." TJ took the toothpick back out of his mouth and put it in the front pocket of his bibs. "Heart attack?"

"I'm sorry to say that it looks like a homicide." The words stabbed my heart as they left Spencer's mouth.

Tears welled up in my eyes. My throat caught a frog in it. No amount of swallowing was going to get rid of it. My nostrils flared as I tried to bite back crying.

"You mean to tell me that someone killed Fred?" TJ reached for a crisp and stuck it in his mouth. His appetite was not too bothered by the death of his neighbor.

"It appears that way, TJ." Spencer drew his eyes down to me. "Can I talk to you first, Roxy?"

"Sure." I nodded.

TJ took the plate from me before I followed Spencer to a spot a little ways from where Fred's body was found. Pepper followed and laid down by my feet.

There was a small puddle of fresh blood. I tried not to look.

"What exactly happened here?" he asked.

The other members of the department worked around the crime scene collecting what looked to be evidence and taking all sorts of pictures. Another man had tied some of the crime scene tape around the trunk of one of the apple trees and walked in front of it as he marked off the crime scene.

"I'd forgotten to pay Fred for my apples I'd gotten from the Farmer's Market, so I drove out here to give him the money and some of the crisps I'd made with his apples. I saw Louise's car in the lot. Naturally I went into the shop he has in the barn and they weren't there." My lip curled in at the thought of what happened next. "Pepper took off toward the orchard, so I thought I'd find them here. It was then that I found Louise standing over his body," I gulped, "holding the knife."

He ran his hand through his hair.

"You know this doesn't look good." He tilted his head.

"Yeah. The fight I saw between them at the market and how he came to Pet Palace to confront her over coming on his property." I grimaced.

"Did she say anything to you before we got here?" Spencer slightly frowned.

"No. She was visibly upset." I nodded, imagining how she must've felt when she found him. "I know how bad it looks, but you can't possibly think Louise did this. She's much smaller than him."

"We'll see." Spencer wrote in his notebook. I stood there while he did. He looked up and motioned for Louise to join us.

Louise fidgeted with her finger. She brushed down her clothes, tucked back her hair and even rocked back and forth on her heels.

"Are you okay?" Spencer asked.

She shot him a withering glance. "Okay? No I'm not okay. It's not every day you happen upon a dead body. Especially one you know."

"Why were you here?" he asked her a very good question, the answer to which I was even interested in.

"I was going to settle our argument once and for all." Her chin thrust down with a definitive nod.

Spencer and I both looked at each other.

"Oh you know what I mean. I didn't come here to kill anyone and I didn't." She protested our looks. "I might as well tell ya." She huffed. "Bertie, Fred's chicken was from Pet Palace. It took me a long time to place her, but Fred took her. He also informed me she's some type of rare chicken and the eggs can sell for hundreds of dollars to the finest restaurants." The muscles in her jaw quivered. "I let him adopt Bertie. Not the eggs that she laid. And it ain't like she can't lay more."

"Bertie had eggs before Fred adopted her?" Spencer asked.

"She did. She had six eggs." Her brows rose. "That's six hundred dollars that I could possibly get for Pet Palace. I need the money. Funds are low and I have to pay Jeremy somehow. Shoot." She scuffed the toe of her shoe in the gravel. "I don't even know how Fred found out."

"What happened when Fred asked you about it?" Spencer continued to write down everything Louise was saying.

"The first time he saw me on the boardwalk. I was taking a new pet to The Bean Hive for the week," she started.

"What day was that?" he asked.

"Last Monday. I take all the animals to Roxy," she pointed to me, "on Monday. And he was taking her some fruit."

"That's right," I agreed when Spencer looked over at me. "I get fruit deliveries on Monday, except when the Farmer's Market opens, which was yesterday."

I wanted to make sure they were very clear on the timeline. I had a niggling suspicion that Spencer was already suspecting Louise as the killer and I just couldn't imagine that.

"What did he say to you when he saw you on the boardwalk?" Spencer turned back to Louise.

"He said that he'd heard that Bertie had laid eggs. I didn't deny it. That's when he insisted the eggs were rightfully his because he adopted Bertie." The more she told the story, the further up her shoulders got to her ears and the stress hung on her face. "I wasn't about to give him the eggs. The adoption papers strictly say Bertie. Nothing was mentioned about eggs. I told him to keep her in the coop and she'd produce more."

"What kind of chicken is Bertie?" Spencer asked.

"She's a rare Ayam Cemani." The breed rolled off her tongue.

"And how do you spell that?" Spencer looked at her from underneath his brows.

While Louise gave Spencer the correct spelling, I typed it into my phone. I'd never heard of such a thing, even in all my years in being a lawyer—granted that was in the city. But if this was some sort of rare bird, then maybe the real killer (because I refused to believe Louise would ever hurt someone) knew about the bird.

"They can fetch up to twenty-five hundred dollars." Louise nodded.

That got Spencer's attention.

"I thought you said a few hundred dollars?" He flipped back through his little notebook to see what he'd written down earlier.

"I said the eggs, not the actual bird. And that's what I told Fred. He's lucky I didn't know what kind of chicken she was when I let him adopt her." Her right brow arched. "I'd probably have done one of those online auctions to get more money for Pet Palace."

"When was the next time you saw him?" Spencer decided to move on to the next confrontation.

We all shuffled into the shade. The afternoon sun was at its hottest and was beating down on the orchard.

"He showed up at Pet Palace when I wasn't there. Jeremy said that Fred was demanding to see the eggs." She held her hand over her brows to shield the sun as she twisted to look at the officers walking around and collecting whatever evidence they could find. "Jeremy told him he didn't know what he was talking about, which he didn't because I didn't tell anyone since I wasn't really sure on how to get rid of the eggs."

"Where are the eggs now?" Spencer asked.

"They are at my house. I dared Fred to come there." Her eyes narrowed. "Not that I'd kill him," she tried to save herself. "The next time I saw him was yesterday at the market. I didn't think he'd say anything, but he did under his breath. I just couldn't take it anymore. Especially after he sic'd his lawyer on me."

Spencer's head jerked up and he looked at her.

"He had a lawyer?" he asked.

"Yep. Going to sue me." She gulped. She brought her hand to her mouth. "Oh goodness. All of this does make me look guilty. I swear I didn't kill him. You do believe me, don't you?"

Interesting that Spencer didn't answer her.

"Take me to today," he suggested.

"The lawyer scared me. If he sued me, Pet Palace would definitely go under. So, I was going to come out here and try to make a deal. I'd give him half the eggs and call it good, but," her voice faded and her eyes slid over to the spot where Fred's body was found, "it looked like someone else had different plans for him."

"Just tell me what happened today." Spencer shifted his weight to his left hip.

"When I couldn't find him in his orchard shop in his barn, I figured he was pulling apples. I walked back here and when I saw him lying on the ground, I immediately bent down to feel for a pulse. That's when I saw the knife. I picked it up and that's when Roxy called my name." She looked at me.

"That's when I called you," I finished up the rest of the story.

"You. . .you believe me right?" Louise looked alarmed.

"Of course I do." Spencer looked very sympathetic. "I'll be in touch."

"I'll talk to you later." I ran a hand down Louise's arm.

She nodded. A tear fell down her face. She quickly wiped it away and darted off toward her car.

I let out a deep sigh of relief to hear Spencer say he believed her. My phone chirped a text. It was from Aunt Maxi. She reminded me of the Beautification Committee meeting in the afternoon that I'd completely forgotten about.

"Well? What do you think happened?" I asked, wondering if he had any more ideas.

"Not sure. But everything points to her." He made a few notes in his little notebook.

"But you said you believed her." I reminded him.

"To an extent I believe her. I don't think she wanted to harm anyone nor do I think there was any sort of premeditation." He shrugged.

"You really think she killed him?" My brows drew together.

"I'm not saying that either. I want to go see Jeremy about the confrontation between him and Fred." Spencer flipped his notebook shut. "Listen, I know Louise is a good friend of yours, but I don't want you to go sniffing around where you shouldn't be. Please, leave this to me and my department."

"Are you referring to Alexis Roarke?" I asked about the last murder investigation in Honey Springs when it just so happened that I'd done a little sleuthing on my own and found the killer.

"Yes." He looked at me with big eyes.

"I stumble across things. What can I say?" I wasn't about to promise anything. "Besides, I'm not snooping when people talk to me. I can't close my ears when people are talking in the coffeehouse."

"Good point. Just don't go looking for answers." His voice was stern. "Got it?"

I stood silent because I didn't want to lie.

"How is your mother?" He changed the subject and walked me and Pepper back to our car.

"Mom," I gasped. I'd completely forgotten about her being in town. "I'm not sure. I better check on her." I gave him a wave, pulled my phone out of my back pocket and patted for Pepper to get into the car.

CHAPTER SEVEN

On our way back to the boardwalk, Pepper stood on the armrest of the passenger side door with his head stuck out of the window. My mind wandered all over the place. I'd had no idea Pet Palace was running low on donations. There were some people on the Beautification Committee that I could talk to about Pet Palace because they also volunteered there. Maybe they'd heard something.

I'd also tried to call my mom, but she still didn't answer so I used the opportunity to call Patrick.

"Hey there." The sound of his voice put a smile on my face.

"I'm so glad you answered." Suddenly my eyes teared. The emotion of what happened to Fred was bubbling up in my throat. "Fred Hill is dead."

"Really?" Patrick said not in a questionable way, but a shocked sort of tone. "That's terrible."

"That's not the bad part. He was murdered." The words left my mouth and my stomach dropped.

"My gosh, by who?" he asked.

"Not sure. Louise Carlton found him before I found her standing over his body with the knife in her hand." I gulped back more tears.

"Don't tell me that you were there before Spencer." There was silence. "Roxy."

"You told me not to tell you," I simply stated. "I went out there because I realized I never paid for the apples we'd gotten from the Farmer's Market and that's when I found Louise standing over him."

"Did they arrest her?"

"Arrest who?" I asked.

"Louise?"

"No. She didn't kill him." How could he possibly think that? "She was out there to make peace with him. It's a long story."

"Why don't you tell me over dinner on the lake and some fishing tonight?" he asked. My heart jumped. Some alone time was probably exactly what I needed. "Your mom said she'd love it if that's what you wanted to do."

"My mom?" There went our alone time.

"Yeah. She called me this morning and asked me to take her to a car rental place so she could rent a car."

"She called you and not me?" I asked.

"She said you were busy with work and she didn't want to bother you." He made her sound like a saint, which she wasn't. "She's going to be an awesome mother-in-law."

I ignored his comment. He'd yet to get to know her.

"Did she say where she was going today because I've called her a few times and she's not answered," I said trying to be cordial.

She was avoiding me and I knew it. She didn't want to be alone with me to answer my questions of where she'd been the past couple of years. Yes. Couple of years. Not to mention how I had to text her because she wouldn't answer her phone calls because after I told her I was going to stop practicing law to open a coffee shop in Honey Springs, she'd nearly lost it on me.

"She said she had a few errands to run. That's all. So what about tonight?" he asked.

"Yeah. Dinner and fishing is fine." What happened to my plan of me getting to know him and not him getting to know my mother. I groaned. "I've got my Beautification Committee right now at All About The Details. After that I'm going back to the coffeehouse to finish up the rest of the day. What time did you tell Mom for tonight?"

"How about seven at my house?" he questioned.

"Perfect." I grinned to myself and pulled into the parking lot of the boardwalk.

When Mom found out that the house that Patrick owned was Aunt Maxi's house when I was a teenager and visited her, she'd see why I fell in love with Honey Springs. After all, she hates Honey Springs and I couldn't help but think that was the source of all our issues.

Boats were coming in and out of marina, the boat dock and boat shop located underneath the pier. There were hundreds of boat slips where boaters stored their boats during the off season. Many of them rented cabins on the lake for the summer or actually owned a cabin. The people I'd bought my cabin from were summer citizens, as we liked to call them.

People were walking all along the boardwalk enjoying the summer day. Laughter filled the holler of the lake and bounced off the limestone walls as children and adults were jumping in and swimming. For a few minutes Pepper and I stopped and watched. It put a big smile on my face and brought back a lot of fond memories of when I was the same age as the kids.

All the shops looked to be busy. The first shop on the boardwalk was Wild and Whimsy Antiques. I'd gotten a lot of the items for the coffeehouse in there. All of my china cups and some of the older antique pieces came from there. The owners, Bev and Dan Teagarden, were always on the lookout for the perfect item for the coffeehouse. The Honey Comb Salon was next to the antique shop.

I peeked my head in to get my friend Crissy Lane's attention. Her lips were flapping a mile a minute while she snipped and curled her client's hair.

"Hey, girl! I'm looking forward to tonight," she called over the chatter of the gossip going on in there with all the women in the chairs.

"I can't make it." I frowned. "But Leslie wants to go, so go talk to her."

"Whatever." Crissy waved her scissors in the air and snarled.

"Be nice. She's trying." Leslie had thought she was too big for her britches when she first came back to lay her mom to rest. She'd not grown up in Honey Springs, but she was giving it a go now so it was time for us to move on and let her in.

"Fine." Crissy looked at me with a flat look.

I laughed and headed on back down the boardwalk. The fries from Buzz In and Out Diner smelled so good. Pepper even stuck his nose up to the window of the diner.

"I'm hungry too," I said to Pepper as we passed. "But we've got to get to the meeting."

With no more dilly-dallying we quickly made our way down to All About the Details. It was the only event planning store in Honey Springs. They not only planned events, but they also hosted them in the shop. It was the biggest shop on the boardwalk. Of course it had to be if it hosted weddings. With the backdrop of Lake Honey Springs, it was a perfect wedding spot.

"Roxy!" Aunt Maxi was standing in the front, waving her arms above her head. Her hair was standing up, hairsprayed to high-heaven. She wore a floral printed caftan over a pair of white skinny jeans and white tank top. A color beaded necklace around her neck. "Over here!"

I waved and smiled, taking a step forward but abruptly stopped when someone else called my name.

"Roxanne! You-whoooo!" My mother stood on the opposite side of the room, drumming her fingers in the air. When she noticed that I saw her, she waved me over.

"Roxy! Here!" Aunt Maxi's words were louder and much harder than they were earlier. "I've got your normal spot!" Aunt Maxi pointed.

"Here, Roxanne!" Mom straightened her shoulders as she glared at Aunt Maxi.

"Here!" Aunt Maxi stomped her foot and fisted her hands next to her sides.

"Or you can sit here." Mae Belle Donovan chirped from a seat in the row I was standing next to. She pulled the floppy straw hat off her chin-length grey hair that was neatly parted to the side. She reached over into the empty chair, pulling her black pocketbook into her lap. Lightly she tapped the empty seat.

I pointed to it for clarification. Mae Belle nodded and I sat down before Mom or Aunt Maxi could protest.

"Thank you," I sat down in the seat and Pepper sat under my chair.

"Ah oh." Mae Belle grimaced. "Which one is going to pee on you first." Mae Belle joked at Mom and Aunt Maxi trying to beat each other to the open seat next to me.

"Got it! Got it first!" My mother plopped down in the chair. Her legs flew up in the air. She huffed and puffed, hugging her purse to her chest.

Aunt Maxi glared at her, glazed over me and stared at Mae Belle. She jerked her head to the side giving Mae Belle the you better scoot down a seat or you'll regret it look.

"Guess I'm moving," Mae Belle whispered in my ear before she scooted.

Aunt Maxi didn't spare no time in getting down to the nitty gritty.

"Well I'm glad to see Penny has come to Honey Springs after all these years," her voice was much louder than it needed to be. "Seems like she's just twenty years too late."

"If you didn't make it so hard to be part of the Bloom family, then I might've come." Mom harrumphed and crossed her arms across her chest.

Neither of them looked at the other.

"You couldn't warn me she was visiting?" Aunt Maxi nudged me.

"Oww." I grabbed my rib. "That's going to leave a bruise."

"We wouldn't be in this situation if you'd told me about her." Aunt Maxi poked her finger in my rib this time, causing me to bump into my mother. She was like a flame to the wood. Mom was the wood.

"If you didn't act like her mother instead of her aunt, we wouldn't be in this situation." The wood caught fire and the flame shot out in front of me.

"If you were ever a mother." Aunt Maxi and Mom went nose-to-nose in front of me.

"Whoa." I pushed them apart. "What is wrong with you two? I love you both. Aunt Maxi was wonderful to me when I was here visiting, but the other nine months out of the year, you were a wonderful mother."

My head turned back and forth between the two.

"Mom, what are you doing here?" I asked.

"Yeah. What she said." Aunt Maxi scowled and pointed to me. "Honey Springs wasn't good enough for you when my brother was living. Why you here now?"

"This is getting good," Mae Belle cackled from next to Aunt Maxi.

"Hush your mouth." Aunt Maxi's anger turned on Mae Belle.

"I won't do it." Mae Belle pushed herself up to standing. She put a hand on her hip and cocked it to the side. "You don't run this town. If you want to know how Penny Bloom found out about the Beautification Committee, then you can talk to me."

"Yes." My mother nodded and smiled. "My soon-to-be son-in-law was precious enough to give me a ride to your charming coffeehouse. Mae Belle was there and she just took right to me."

"She did, did she?" Aunt Maxi's eyes zeroed in on Mae Belle Donovan.

It was no secret that Mae Belle and Aunt Maxi have had words a time or two over silly little things and gossip. Aunt Maxi poked Mae Belle. "You did, did you?"

Mae Belle whacked Aunt Maxi with her floppy hat.

"You better hold on one cotton pickin' minute." Mae Belle continued to whack Aunt Maxi over the head until Aunt Maxi started flailing her hands back at Mae Belle.

"Stop it right this minute." I jumped up and parted the two of them.

"See," Aunt Maxi ran her fingers in her spiky hair. "See the fuss you caused." She directed her words to Mom. "You make a mess everywhere you go!"

Aunt Maxi pushed past our chairs and darted out the door but not without saying a few words that'd make the devil blush.

When I looked up, all of the committee members had turned around and were watching everything that had gone on.

"And that's why I never came here. I never knew when she was going to go off half-cocked." Mom seemed pleased as a peach that Aunt Maxi had left. She put her hand in the crook of my arm and shimmied her hiney in the chair closer to me.

I sucked in a deep breath and offered a sweet smile to everyone who was still staring.

"Now if I can have your attention now that the soap opera has come to an end." Alice Dee Spicer's lines creased her forehead as her brows dipped when she looked directly at me. "We've gotten the new banners for all the carriage lights, so if we could have a volunteer that'd be great."

Mom's hand shot up. She waved her hand.

"Penny? Are you sure?" Alice's face was flawless and her makeup was on point. Her brown hair was layered and glossy, not to mention, styled to perfection.

Which it should be since she owned Honey Comb hair salon. Recently, she'd been voted in as the president of the Beautification Committee after our last president had been sent to jail for killing Alexis. Alice was the perfect choice since she was already the vice president. We'd yet to fill her vacant position. I wasn't going to suggest any nominees.

"Of course, I'm excited to get to know my new home." Mom's words caused me to jump up, because she obviously didn't understand what Alice was saying.

"Wait." I held my hand in the air. I bent down and whispered into my mom's ear. "She's asking for a member of the committee to have a full-time position of doing banners since it was her job as our vice president. Not just while you are here visiting."

"Visiting?" Mom chuckled. "I'm not visiting." She looked down at her watch and gave it a good tap with her fingernail. "In fact, I've got to go because I'm going to see a house to buy." She stood up, leaving me with my mouth gaped open. My limp body sat back down into the chair. "I'd love to do it and take over the position. I'll see you at Honey Comb at six."

What was going on? My mind tried to wrap around what was happening. My mom took a step out of the aisle. She looked over her shoulder.

"Toodles. I'll see you later." She trotted out the door of All About the Details, leaving me dumbfounded.

"Your mom is a sight." Mae Belle looked to be enjoying every bit of the idea that my mom was in town. She rubbed her hands together. "She's going to drive Maxine Bloom plum crazy and I'm going to be sipping on my sweet tea watching it all." She smiled. "Or coffee. Coffee is good too."

"I'm not sure what's going on." I gnawed on my bottom lip. "But I don't have time to worry about that. Do you know where I can get some good apples?"

"Hill's Orchard of course," she said.

"I hate to give you the bad news, but Fred Hill is dead. Someone killed him." Images of Louise standing over Fred rolled around in my memory. I shivered.

"What? Fred Hill was murdered?" Her voice carried over the meeting. There was a collective gasp that filled the room.

CHAPTER EIGHT

"*D*on't tell me that you found another body?" Aunt Maxi sat on one of the stools at the island in the kitchen of The Bean Hive. Tank was curled up in her lap fast asleep.

"Let's just say that I found Louise standing over his body." My brows drew together. "Oh darn. How many scoops was that?"

I looked at the whole beans of coffee in the sack with the scoop in my hand, then I looked at the cinnamon scoop. I'd completely lost count of my ratio. Many of my customers had asked how I make the cinnamon blend that I served and so I got the bright idea to package it to sell. Ever since then, it'd been flying off the shelves.

"You mean to tell me that Louise killed Fred?" Bunny asked when she came in the swinging kitchen door from the shop in the middle of the conversation. Pepper followed behind her.

I flipped him a homemade dog treat from the jar that sat on the island. He grabbed it and took it back to his bed.

"I didn't say that at all." I dumped the contents of what I'd already made up and started from scratch. "Can you grab those mini hot browns out of the oven and plate them for the late afternoon lunch crowd?"

"Fred was awfully hard to get along with. Didn't Louise and Fred have a fight at the Farmer's Market?" Bunny pulled on a pair of oven mitts.

The smell of oozing cheese, warm bread, and ham created a heavenly scent as the steamed rolled out from the warm oven. Without even trying to, we all smiled and sighed. It was amazing what food did for the soul once it was eaten, but it was the smell that hooked them. My little secret was to bake something daily in a small pewter dish and set it in the air duct. When the air conditioner kicked on, the entire coffeehouse smelled of something delicious. It never failed that customers always asked what smelled so good.

"Yeah. Not to mention he'd come in Pet Palace demanding to see her when I was volunteering the other night." I looked over the hot browns. Each little mini one was browned perfectly with the creamy sauce bubbling up around the outsides. If my stomach weren't in knots over not only the reason for Fred's death, but also Mom's sudden urge to move to Honey Springs, I might've eaten one.

I took a couple of them off the baking sheet and put them on the cooling rack. They were perfect for a single meal and I wanted to take Jean Hill a couple along with my condolences.

"So it's not looking good for Louise?" Aunt Maxi asked.

"What do you mean, he was awfully hard to get along with?" I asked. "He'd always been nice to me."

"He was nice to you because you bought from him." Bunny looked at Aunt Maxi. "Whatever happened between him and TJ?"

"You know." Aunt Maxi looked out into the kitchen as if she were studying something. "I never heard."

"TJ Holmes? The neighbor?" I recalled the man that'd come over to the crime scene.

Aunt Maxi nodded. "From what I remember, Doris Blankenship sold TJ the property next to Fred and I'd heard that she convinced TJ to have the land surveyed and part of Fred's apple orchard was on his property."

"And TJ tried to strike a deal with Fred that he'd lease the land to him or something like that." Bunny *tsked*, "Oh, my mind must be going because I can't keep all that straight."

"Who told you about all this?" I asked.

"It's all public knowledge and a little bit of gossip. Ida Combs is the clerk at the courthouse and she was telling book club about it." Bunny shrugged and pushed through the swinging door butt first with the tray of mini hot browns in her hand.

"Book club?" Inquisitively I looked over at Aunt Maxi and put in the last scoop of cinnamon. "If I'd known there was a book club, I'd have joined *it* rather than the Beautification Committee."

I turned on the coffee grinder and pulled empty coffee bags with The Bean Hive logo from underneath the island.

"You'll have to ask Leslie about it. I think they still meet in Crooked Cat, but I'm not for sure." Her voice rose above the grinder. "Speaking of Beatification Committee."

I took a deep breath to prepare myself for what I knew was coming next. Questions about

Mom.

"Why didn't you tell me that Penny was in town?" she asked in a calm manner that I could tell she was trying so hard to maintain.

"I had no idea she was coming to town. I've not talked to her in months. When Spencer dropped me off the other night, she was sitting in one of my rocking chairs." I poured some ground cinnamon coffee into each bag before I ran the seal around the edges.

"Spencer?" Aunt Maxi questioned. "Why were you with Spencer?"

"Long story short, I'd fallen asleep during my volunteering at Pet Palace. He saw the light on later than usual and decided to stop by. It was too late for me and Pepper to ride the bike back so Spencer gave us a ride." Why was it so hard to believe that the members of the opposite sex could be friends these days? "Anyways, after I got in the house and ready to question Mom, she was fast asleep on the couch and she was still asleep this morning."

"You still could've warned me." Aunt Maxi was going to beat it and run over it until she was satisfied. She put Tank on the ground. The little fellow yawned and stretched.

"I didn't know how long she was going to be in town." I finished sealing all the bags and stacked them in my arms. "You know her. She's got a mind of her own. She always up and left with little to no notice."

I headed into the coffeehouse with Aunt Maxi, Tank, and Pepper on my heels.

"I was just as taken aback as you when I saw her here." I put the bags of coffee on the display case on the right wall of the shop. "I'm not even sure where's she's been. I guess when I find out from her, I'll tell you."

The rest of the afternoon was spent cleaning and restocking the glass cases. Over the last couple of months, I'd hired a couple of the high school girls to run the coffeehouse from the afternoon hours to closing time. They'd come as a recommendation from the Home Economics teacher from Honey Springs High after I'd gone to the school to post a Help Wanted ad.

Not only did it give me a much-needed break, it also gave me a good peace of mind the shop was running smoothly.

"Any questions?" I asked Emily Rich, the one of the two girls who was more interested in the baking part of the job.

"Nope." She smiled and brushed her long brown hair behind her shoulders.

"Do you have any questions?" I asked Katrina, the other girl that was more interested in the business side of the job.

"No, ma'am. If we do, we'll call." Katrina's blond hair was cut shoulder length, but was pulled back in two braids. "Have a great date."

"I'll take Pepper and Tank out several times." Emily had really taken to Pepper. He loved her too.

Patrick had been trying to get me to go away for a long weekend, but I'd been hesitant because of Pepper and the shop. Now I didn't have any excuses and thought about bringing up a long weekend tonight when we were together.

Confident everything was going well, I quickly changed my work clothes into a pair of shorts and tee since Patrick and I were going to go fishing. I'd tried to call my mom a couple of times, but she didn't answer or return my call. I had a sneaky suspicion she was avoiding me.

I went out on the boardwalk and stood there looking out over Lake Honey Springs. The sun was starting to go down behind the tree line and a light summer breeze skidded across the calm water.

It was a good time to call Spencer and let him know what I'd found out.

"What's going on?" he answered the phone. "You've not come across any more dead bodies have you?"

"That's not even funny," I joked and leaned up against the railing of the boardwalk with my back to the lake. "I did find out that Fred also had a beef with his neighbor TJ Holmes."

"Yeah. I'd heard about that months ago, and after I let you and Louise leave the orchard, he was still hanging around. I asked him about that lawsuit and he said that it'd been settled in Honey Springs Courthouse months ago. Plus, he has an alibi at the time of death." Spencer continued to tell me about how the coroner had come back with a time of death, which was about twenty minutes before I'd gotten there.

"If I'd only gotten there a half hour earlier," I said.

"I'm glad you didn't or you might be dead." His words struck home. "I finally got in touch with his wife. She was away at her sister's for the night. The strawberries they didn't sell at the Farmer's Market, she took to her sister's to make homemade jams. She's pretty devastated."

"I couldn't imagine." Really I couldn't. My mind turned to Patrick. After all these years we finally found each other again, I couldn't imagine losing him now. I gulped and changed the subject. "What did you say TJ's alibi was?"

"He's a mechanic and does all the work for the marina. He was down there working on the boats of some summer citizens. You know boats." He hesitated. "They sit all winter and need to be worked on. TJ is a busy man the first couple of weeks of the summer because everyone wants their boats worked on first."

"Not that I wanted TJ to be the killer, but I sure wish there was someone other than Louise," I said and looked down the boardwalk.

"Like I said, you let me handle all the investigative work, but if you do hear something, please call me." We hung up the phone just as another call was coming in.

It was from the landline at Pet Palace.

"Hello," I answered not sure if it was Louise or Jeremy, her fulltime employee.

"Thank goodness you answered," Louise's voice cracked. "I really think I'm in trouble and I didn't know who to turn to."

"Louise." A knot the size of a goose egg felt like it was lodged in my throat. "Please don't tell me that you did kill Fred Hill."

"For goodness sakes, no," her voice dripped through the phone. "They think I did. That's my problem. Spencer told me there aren't any other suspects and that I'm the one everyone says had a bad relationship with him recently."

"Did he say that you are his number one suspect?" I asked, knowing that it didn't take someone with a law degree like me to figure it out. All the evidence did point to her.

"He didn't say that in so many words. He said not to leave town." She breathed heavily into the phone.

"Calm down and catch your breath. There's no sense in getting all worked up until. . ."

"Until what, Roxy? Until he's got me locked up in the county pen?" She wasn't being very reasonable at the moment and who could blame her.

"What did you need my help in doing?" I asked.

"I need you to be my lawyer. There ain't nobody in Honey Springs as smart as you." If she thought flattery was going to work on me, she was right. "If they put me in jail for a crime I didn't commit, what would happen to the animals? I've seen something like this before."

"Someone at a shelter went to jail for murder?" I wondered if I could find that case in the library. It was how lawyers did structure their cases, by looking up similar cases and seeing the outcome, then tweaking it to their case.

"No. Other shelters being shut down and the animals shipped off to who knows where. Maybe animal mills for breeding. Not to mention that you helped solve Alexis's murder."

"Louise, I adore you." The thought of Pet Palace and all the animals going to different shelters broke my heart. "I'm more than happy to help. But I'm not sure if my admission to the Kentucky Bar Association has been approved." I'd kind of dropped the ball on that after Aunt Maxi was no longer a suspect in Alexis Roarke's death. "I'll have to go down to the clerk's office at the courthouse to check."

"You'll do that for little ole me?" Now that she had her way, her southern charm had returned.

"I can't promise I'll find anything out. I'm not a detective and I certainly don't know how to solve crimes." Not that being a lawyer wasn't part of sleuthing because it was.

In the distance, I could see Patrick at the far end of the boardwalk near Wild and Whimsy. I told him I'd meet him at his boat slip at the marina. He disappeared down the ramp to the boat dock.

"Let me look around and see what I can find out." I assured her, "I'll even go by the courthouse to see what the status on my paperwork is."

As a lawyer, you couldn't just plop down in any town and start taking clients. There was a whole process with paperwork, certification and it varied from state to state.

I started walking toward the marina when we said our goodbyes.

The cottage style building floated on Lake Honey Springs with the rest of the boat dock and slips. It was charming and looked like it used to be a lake house. There was an awning over the front glass door. The flip sign was flipped to the open side.

Though I knew Patrick was probably already on his boat in his slip, my curiosity of TJ doing work for Big Bib and the summer citizens tugged on me. It wasn't like Spencer didn't know what he was talking about, but phooey! Louise was on the hook and I'd promised to look into it.

Looking into it didn't mean that I was actually digging in deep and trying to find clues to get her off the suspect list. It meant that I'd keep my ears open to what people were saying. Gossip in Honey Springs was a way of life whether you were looking for it or not.

The marina was a typical boat shop and general store like most lakes had. Big Bib sold the boating essentials like fire extinguishers, life jackets, floats, fishing equipment, boat batteries, beer, snacks, coolers, koozies, and much more. He knew exactly how to cater to the summer citizens and his prices reflected that he knew he was the only place in town to get this stuff.

"Hey, Roxy." Big Bib stood at the register, focusing on the television that was always on the Weather Channel.

He claimed that he was tired of boaters coming in and asking what the weather was going to be, so now he just pointed to the TV he'd hung on the wall.

"Looks like it's going to be a great weekend for boaters." He nodded.

"It sure does." I perused the candy aisle like I was looking for something.

"Your boy's already been in here and grabbed some chocolates to go with that fancy wine he had." Big Bib turned his attention to me. He was a big burly man. He had on a pair of jeans, a sleeveless Metallica shirt that he'd cut the sleeves off of and a pair of red suspenders clipped on the waist of his jeans.

I smiled. Patrick was really going out of his way to make tonight special.

"Is Steve still working here?" I asked.

"Why you want to know?" Big Bib had always been tight lipped under that full beard of his.

"I met TJ Holmes and he said that he's been down here working on summer citizens' boats and I thought that was Steve's job." I shrugged and walked over to the counter.

"TJ is a motor man. He pulls the boats out and works on them at his place. Most of his work is done during the winter months when boaters don't need their boats. Sometimes I have an emergency that Steve can't fix and we need a mechanic like TJ, but not lately."

"He wasn't here yesterday?" I wondered because he told Spencer that he was at the marina and that was his alibi. Or was it?

"Naw." Big Bib smirked. "He called and said if the fuzz came snooping around to tell them he was here." He's brows narrowed. "You aren't the fuzz are you?"

"Me? A cop?" I *tsked*.

I wanted to say, *no, but I'm going to tell the cops.*

"Why on earth would he be trying to hide from the cops?" I snorted, hoping my reaction would come off in a not caring kind of way.

"TJ hasn't always had the best record when it comes to keeping clean. He's been arrested for selling pot, smoking pot, even eating pot in some food. He's harmless and they're always on him for weed. He don't bother me none as long as he gets his work done. He's the best around here." He grabbed the phone as soon as it rang.

I gave a slight wave and headed out the door. If TJ wasn't where he said he was, where was he? Stabbing Fred Hill because of their lawsuit? Spencer said that TJ said the lawsuit had been settled. He also told Spencer he was working at the Marina. Before I told Spencer that TJ was a liar, I'd check out the paperwork at the courthouse tomorrow when I went to check on my license.

"There you are." Patrick held a hand out for me to take to help me on the boat.

It was a pontoon with bench seating on each side of the front of the boat and a long bench seat along the back with a removable table. In the middle was the steering shaft and a captain's chair.

He didn't waste any time pulling me into his arms and showing me just how much he loved me.

"What did I do to deserve all of this?" I asked and looked at all the bags from The Watershed on the floor.

The Watershed was a fancy restaurant on the boardwalk. They had beautiful views of the lake from their tables and they also did dinner cruises. The prices were steep and it was only special occasions that brought us there to eat.

He handed me a life jacket.

"You're my number one gal." He helped me snap it across my chest and proceeded to untie the rope knots that tied us to the boat dock. "You want to know things I love as a man." He winked on his way back to the captain's chair where he started up the engine and began to back the boat out of the slip. "I love spending any time with you."

I didn't question him. The time was special. My insides felt like one of the snow globes that'd just been shaken up. The glitter was fluttering inside of me and my heart soared. How on earth could I ever think we weren't meant to be together?

I stood up behind him with my hands on his shoulders and kneaded them as we putted along the no wake zone. As soon as we hit the buoys that marked the end of the no wake zone, he shoved the gearshift up and the pontoon went full speed. I closed my eyes and let the wind whip away all of the day's stress.

After a few minutes, the motor of the boat slowed to a low hum as Patrick pulled back on the gearshift and drove us into a cove with a small waterfall at the end. The trickle of the water was so soothing as it ran across the limestone.

"This is beautiful." I sat down and enjoyed the relaxation of the boat as it swayed back and forth while Patrick threw out the anchor.

"Nothing is a beautiful as you." The lines around his eyes deepened as the smile traveled toward them. "I hope you like what I ordered for you. But I want you to go up there and sit on the edge of the boat with your toes in the water while I get the table set."

"You won't hear any complaints out of me." I got up and slipped off my shoes doing exactly what he asked me to do.

Though I loved owning The Bean Hive, I took my customer's needs into consideration with everything I baked and cooked and brewed. There was a little bit of pressure to please everyone who entered the coffeehouse. It was nice to take these couple of hours and be waited on by Patrick.

Lake Honey Springs was crystal clear and warm. The tips of my toes barely skimmed the top of the water from the boat's edge. The lake was down a little for this time of the year since the warm summer months seemed to dry everything out. During the spring and fall months we had to worry about the rising waters and flooding.

Since I only visited during the summer months, I'd never seen a real flood, only heard of it. And now that I lived here, I hoped I'd never have to witness such a tragedy in the community.

"Here you go." Patrick's arm came over my shoulder as he handed me a glass of wine. "Enjoy while I get supper on the table."

"Why don't you sit here with me and enjoy a glass?" I asked.

"I'd love to." He headed to the back of the boat and filled his glass up. "You want to tell me what you found out about Fred Hill because I know you. And I know that you just aren't going to let Spencer do his job."

I took his glass while he rolled up the bottom of his jeans and sat next to me to put his bare feet into the calm water. The water rippled.

"Not when it comes to Louise. She did ask me to be her lawyer." It was a great excuse for me to use and not look like some nosy lady. I scooted back on the boat deck a little more and drew one leg up as I turned toward Patrick. "I did find out that TJ Holmes lied to Spencer about his alibi."

His eyes frowned in a questioning type of way.

"Yep. He told Spencer he was at the marina fixing a boat motor, but when I got here to meet you, I popped my head into the marina shop where Big Bib was and I asked him in a round about way if TJ was working for him yesterday."

"You really should keep out of this. I can't imagine what I'd do if you got caught in the middle of something." The questioning look had turned into a look of concern.

"I'm going to tell Spencer." Maybe not right away, but eventually after I looked around a little bit, I'd tell him. "Granted, Louise might've been in a public fight with Fred, but TJ had more of a reason."

"What?"

"Money. According to Aunt Maxi and Bunny," Not that I'd consider them the gospel of truth, but they did know a lot. "When TJ bought his house, he had the land surveyed. Part of the actual land that Fred's apple orchard is on is in fact TJ's land. They were in a big lawsuit."

"That's old news." Patrick shoved the gossip to the side. "If I remember correctly, I think TJ had sued and I'm not sure what happened, but I'd heard it was over."

"What do you think happened?" I wondered.

"Obviously, Fred settled and paid TJ." He made sense. "I imagine Fred wasn't about to let go of that orchard."

"How on earth did the land get misaligned?" I took a sip of my wine and dragged a toe through the water to watch it ripple.

"Out there it's more country and when land was sold way back when, they'd walk off the property to what they thought was theirs. That's how they marked it back then." Patrick would know since he grew up in the construction business. "Nowadays, that wouldn't fly. Just like TJ. He probably paid a pretty penny for the land and wanted to make sure he got what was his."

"If you ask me, TJ has more motive than Louise over some dumb eggs." I tipped back the glass and finished off my wine.

"I guess we'd better eat before the sun goes down." He made a good point. "The boat has lights, but it's much more enjoyable when the sun's out."

The relaxation didn't last long. My phone chirped a message from my mother. She wanted to know where I was and when I was coming home. I silenced my phone. I wasn't a teenager anymore even though Patrick made me feel like it.

"Let me guess. Your mom?" Patrick asked from behind me.

"How on earth did you know?" I asked jokingly.

"Dinner is served." He came over to get me.

On the table he'd put out two candlesticks with lit candles and two mismatched china plates with two big burgers and onion rings on them.

"I didn't get plates so I ran over to Wild and Whimsy. Bev said that you'd love these and could use them in the coffeehouse." He was very sweet and efficient.

"She was right. I do love them." I couldn't help but notice one had a blue pattern around the edges while the other had a gold ring. "It'd be perfect for serving a helping of something."

"Tell me about your mom," Patrick said once we sat down to eat.

"Well." I knew that I had to tell him and not be aloof if he was going to be my husband. "I love my mom. I do. But she never wanted to be part of this world. Here in Honey Springs," I clarified. "She and my dad never fought until it came to summers and me. For some reason, she and Aunt Maxi never got along. I've never asked why. Mom said she'd never come to Honey Springs and now she's here. To live?"

"Maybe she just wants a relationship with you," Patrick said.

"She and I were never as close as my father and me. She was gone on business trips and worked a lot." I took a bite out of my burger. It was so good.

"What did she do for a living?" he asked.

"She worked in the IT department of the IRS." I continued to stuff my face.

"Does she still work?" he asked between bites.

"I guess not. I don't know. I've not gotten to have any time with her since she showed up the other night." I took a sip of the wine to clear my palate. "She and Aunt Maxi got into a big ole fight at the Beatification Committee today."

He laughed. "I can imagine Maxi is a wee-bit jealous of anyone besides herself spending time with you."

"She didn't hold back any punches when Mom claimed me as her daughter. You know Aunt Maxi thinks she's my mom." I smiled. "I think I'm lucky to have them both in my life. I just wished they'd get along."

"Maybe our wedding can bring peace to the family." He leaned over and used the napkin to wipe the corner of my mouth. "I love you, Roxy."

"I love you too." My heart melted as his tender and warm lips pressed against mine.

CHAPTER NINE

"*I*'ll never get sick of this view, even in the dark." I stood on the deck at Patrick's house that overlooked Lake Honey Springs. There were enough stars to light up the water on the lake. The full moon made it even more romantic. Even the cicadas singing in the dark night sounded pretty. "Remember how we would spend almost every summer night out here?"

It was hard to not bring up the past and how Aunt Maxi had lived here. It was actually her dream house that she'd built. The last summer I'd stayed with her, the financial market in Honey Springs took a downward spiral. Most of her income was tied up in property and not liquid. The fastest way to keep herself from drowning was to sell her house. At the time I'd no clue what was going on and I thought Patrick's family had just took her house. It was then that I turned my anger toward Patrick Cane and never came back to Honey Springs.

Aunt Maxi visited me several times each year and it wasn't until a few months ago when I'd moved back to Honey Springs did I find out the truth. If Aunt Maxi had to move, I'm thrilled it was Patrick's family who'd bought it. In the end, Patrick had purchased it from his parents.

"Dinner was great," I whispered when he walked up behind me and wrapped his arms around me. "Thank you."

After the wonderful meal, we'd made it back to the boat dock right in time for the sun to set. The girls at the coffeehouse were just closing up when we'd stopped by to get Pepper and put Tank to bed. Emily had left a note saying that she took Tank home and she hoped it was okay. It was absolutely fine. I hated to leave the animals at the coffeehouse all night, but I knew I couldn't take them home with me. While we were there, I'd taken the opportunity to grab some honey donuts out of the freezer and put them in the refrigerator to thaw overnight.

"You're welcome." He squeezed me. "I'm glad you wanted to continue back here."

Pepper and Sassy nudged between us with each end of the same rope toy in their respective mouths. We took a step back away from the deck railing. I bent down and grabbed the middle of the rope toy and tugged to make them both pull harder.

"I would offer you another glass of wine, but your mother keeps calling my phone." He held his phone out to me. "Has she called you?"

A deep sigh escaped me. I shrugged.

"I don't know. I flipped on the silent switch." This was really starting to get on my nerves.

"Maybe you should call her?" he suggested. "She seems worried."

"She's not been worried for years." I shook my head. "Let's go home, Pepper."

There was no use in fighting it. Mom was going to drive me and Patrick crazy until she heard from one of us.

"You can't just call her?" Patrick pouted. He shoved the phone at me.

"If I do, she'll just beg me to come home." I ran my hand down his arm and curled up on my toes to give him a nice kiss.

"So you are going to stay out of the investigation right?" Patrick wanted a confirmation from me after we'd gotten into his car with my bike bolted on the bike rack on the back.

After he realized I was going to bike everywhere like most of the citizens of Honey Springs, he put a bike rack on the back of his car for times like this.

"I'm going to help out my client." I wasn't going to lie to him. "I can't help it if I uncover something."

"Then you will give that information to Spencer?" he asked.

I ho-hummed, knowing he'd take that as a yes, but he couldn't see the look on my face in the dark car.

Like a true southern gentleman, he walked me and Pepper to the porch of my cabin. The light was on, which was something Mom did when I was a teen and out with my friends.

"I have to tell you that the other night when I saw you driving up with Spencer, I got a little jealous." His breath brushed past my ear after he curled me in for a goodnight hug. "I didn't like seeing you with another man."

"It was only Spencer." I hugged him tighter.

"He's single, good looking and not going grey like me." He pulled away and brushed his hand through his hair.

"It only makes you more mature looking and sexy." I grabbed a fist full of shirt and tugged him toward me.

His warm lips met mine, he put his arm around my waist and pulled me tighter.

"Are you sure you can't just call her?" he moaned.

The light flickered and we stepped apart.

"She used to do that when I was a teenager too. I'll call you in the morning." I gave him one last kiss before Pepper and I went into the house where I flipped off the front porch light like I used to when I was a teenager.

CHAPTER TEN

*F*our-thirty in the morning comes awfully early and the effects of trying to figure out who killed Fred, having my mother here, dating my fiancé, and running the coffeehouse had me sagging and dragging.

"Let's go, Pepper." I'd gotten a quick shower, pulled my The Bean Hive logo polo on with a pair of khaki shorts.

It was going to be a warm day, not to mention a busy day. This weekend was going to be packed. I had to get the coffeehouse ready for the start of the tourists arriving.

"Good morning," my mom startled me when I was trying to sneak through the cabin so I wouldn't wake her up.

My mom was already up and fresh as a daisy. She took one of the ceramic coffee mugs off one of the pegs over the coffee maker and poured me a hot cup of steaming coffee. I held the cup up to my nose.

"Do I smell lavender?" I asked.

"Taste it." She encouraged me, taking a step back to see the look on my face.

I brought the cup up to my mouth and took a sip. Without swallowing, I let the warm coffee sit in my mouth so the flavor would melt into my tongue before it slid down my throat.

"Mom, this is delicious." I took a bigger drink and thoroughly enjoyed the hint of lavender.

"You aren't the only one in this family who can make some great coffee." She eased a smile. "In fact, I don't think you remember when you were a little girl and wanted to drink my coffee so badly. Your father insisted you were too small to try it. But you were so smart." She reached out and wrapped one of my curls around her finger. "You said that you had a headache."

"How old was I?" I asked.

"Four or five." She laughed. "Not old enough to know what a headache was, but you'd heard your father say he had headaches and I'd fix him a cup of coffee. It was your way of trying to get coffee. It was so cute. Of course I gave in and let you sip mine." She brought her cup up to her lips and took a drink.

"So I have you to blame for my coffee addiction?" I joked.

"You're welcome, because I can see you are very happy here." She sighed. "You know I only wanted what was best for you. That's why I pushed so hard for law school. As far as Honey Springs, your father used to tell me how most people who grew up in Honey Springs stayed here. I wanted you to see the great big world like I did. Your father was content staying in one place and you are just like him." Her voice cracked, "I miss him so much."

"Where have you been?" I asked. "Where is your new husband?"

That was a sore subject. I'd never met the man. Mom had called and told me she was going to travel the world and had gotten remarried.

"That." Her jaw tensed and she swayed her hip against the counter. She brought her hands up to her chest with her cup nestled between her fingers. "I'm going to shoot straight. I was gone most of the time for work because I was doing IT, but it was for the big Fortune 500 companies. It was during the time the Internet was hitting it big and I was pulling in a lot of money for our family." She looked at me. "Not that it was right, but your father and I agreed that I'd do as many jobs as I could while the iron was hot."

My brows furrowed. I knew what it meant to work all the time.

"Honey, it's all over. I knew that I had to spend more time with you so I took one last assignment overseas and trained my replacement before I took early retirement. I never married, but that's what I had to say so you'd believe I'd just up and run like before."

"Did Dad know?" I asked.

"He did, but not Maxine. She just assumed I was a no account mother who'd go on trips for months and let your father take care of you. It wasn't that I don't like Honey Springs, but during the summer most of the big CEOs would take off. I was able to be home and that's when he'd drag you here."

"After your father passed, I threw myself into my work. I'm not saying it was the right thing, but it helped not being in our home. You were in school, then you got married. When you told me that you were getting divorced, leaving your law practice, and moving here, I knew I didn't want to waste any more time being without you." Her words came out of her mouth and I could see the sadness on her face as her mouth dipped.

"I. . ." I was at a loss for words as I started to digest all of it. "I've got to get to work, but why don't you come down and teach me this lavender coffee." I set the mug on the counter after I took another drink. "Is there some chocolate in there?"

"White chocolate." She tilted her head to the side. Her lips formed a thin line. "Thank you for giving me a place to stay. But I've got a meeting with Doris Blankenship to look at a house, so I can get out of your hair."

She took the travel mug off one of the open shelves next to the sink and filled it with coffee. She handed it to me.

"Take your time." I wanted to tell her that she wasn't going to end my dates anymore and that I was a grown woman, but I figured we'd done enough therapy for four-thirty a.m.

The seven-minute bike ride was refreshing. The air wasn't too humid and there was a little breeze coming off the lake as the fog still hung a few feet above the calm water. The only sounds on the board-walk were from the marina. There was always something going on there. Some of the summer citizens even spent the night on their boats. Big Bib did a lot of business with those customers because they'd buy him out of beer and hang out on the dock drinking until the wee hours of the night. Then he'd come into the coffeehouse and buy up my donuts to sell and serve for breakfast.

I locked my bike in front of the coffeehouse, took Pepper out of the basket and opened the front door. The coffeehouse felt so much like home. I'd put all my heart and soul into it. It not only helped me with my passion in life, it helped heal my broken heart.

I flipped on the lights and turned around to look out the window over Lake Honey Springs. My spirit was light and my heart was no longer heavy when I thought of my mother.

"We are so lucky," I said to Pepper who'd already left my side and danced around his bowl. "Alright, I'll feed you."

On my way back to put some kibble in his bowl, I flipped on all the industrial coffee pots at the coffee stations, but not without thinking how Mom had made that amazing lavender flavor. I'd used lavender in tea before, but never infused my coffee with it.

I headed back to the kitchen and turned on the gas ovens to preheat. There was going to be a lot of baking today and I might as well get to it. I knew the temperature was going to hit in the high eighties and the boardwalk would get hot. Most of the summer citizens brought their family pets to the lake with them, so even though I left out a bowl of fresh water outside of the shop, I decided to make pup-sicles instead of dog treats. There was something special about a my pup-sicles.

I took out of the refrigerator the honey donuts that I'd taken out of the freezer last night when Patrick and I'd stopped by. I'd taken out seven dozen and knew that Big Bib would be here to get at least four.

The bell on the ovens dinged letting me know they'd been preheated. I slid as many baking sheets filled with the honey donuts that I could into them and set the timer. There were four big seedless watermelons in the refrigerator that I needed to use before they went bad and knew they'd be perfect for my pup-sicles.

Pepper jumped up and barked a few times. I pushed out the

swinging kitchen door. Aunt Maxi and my mom were both on the other side of the door, already fussing at each other. They didn't even notice I was there. I tapped my fingernail on the glass. Both of them looked at me.

"I'm not opening this door if you two are going to fuss and fight," I warned them. "This is a safe zone."

Aunt Maxi criss-crossed her finger across her chest and Mom gave the girl-scouts honor. My eyes slid back and forth between them before I unlocked the door, letting them in.

"Lock the door behind you," I said over my shoulder on my way back to the kitchen. There was a scuffle behind me. I stopped and turned around. "Are you actually fighting over who can lock the door first?"

I let out an exhausted sigh and shook my head on the way back into the kitchen. Like two scolded teenage girls, they came in silently and both sat on the stools at the island.

"Mom, can you make a pot of that lavender coffee for us this morning?" I asked.

"Of course, dear." She jumped off the stool and tugged on the edge of her shirt.

Aunt Maxi's mouth dropped open and her eyes narrowed. When she caught me looking at her, she turned her lips up into a huge smile.

"How is Patrick?" she asked.

"He's great. We went out on his boat last night. We were going to go fishing, but it was so romantic that we just enjoyed each other's company until Mom wouldn't stop calling." I grabbed an ice cream scoop from one of the kitchen drawers.

"He's a good boy." Aunt Maxi nodded.

"Can you get me the coconut milk out of the refrigerator?" I asked her. If I kept them busy, maybe they'd get along.

As I scooped out the inside of the watermelon, I went ahead and put it in the blender. I took the coconut milk Aunt Maxi had set next to the blender and added it to the blender. As the blender mixed the two ingredients I used in my pup-sicles, I grabbed industrial ice trays from the freezer and brought them over to the island where I poured the mixture into the trays.

"The animals are going to love those." Aunt Maxi put her hands together. She looked over at my mom as Mom poured three cups of her secret coffee. "Do you want me to get rid of her?" she whispered.

I glared at her as I scooped more watermelon.

The timer on the oven dinged and without telling her, Mom grabbed a couple potholders and took out the donuts.

"If you want to grab three dozen to-go boxes and fill them, that'd be great." I still had to add more honey glaze over top of them, but I'd wait to do that when Big Bib got there so they were super fresh.

As Mom and I worked at the island and Aunt Maxi enjoyed the coffee, I figured it was time to call a truce between all of us.

"I'm only going to say this once. You can choose to listen to me and accept my decision or you cannot accept it and not be part of my life." I looked at Aunt Maxi. "I know you own this building and I might make you mad, but I know you love me and I need you to accept my mom just as she is."

Aunt Maxi's mouth opened to either protest or say something, but I *tsked* her.

"And you know that I love Aunt Maxi more than just as an aunt." My brows cocked when I looked at my mom who'd stopped putting the donuts in the to-go boxes to protest. She closed her mouth. I continued, "My parents loved each other. They raised me to be who I am and both of you love me. My heart and soul is right here in this building. All of you, Pepper, and my shop." I bit back the tears as I realized my life was really starting to be the life I'd always dreamed of. "Regardless of Mom's job, she's retired and here now. She's loving Honey Springs as much as I do."

"Can I say something?" Mom put her hand in the air like she was in kindergarten. "I was jealous that you got to spend the summers with my daughter, but I'm grateful at the same time because it gave me time to spend alone with my husband that I'm eternally thankful for." She reached across the island and put her hand on Aunt Maxi's.

"I'd love to take you to lunch and explain where I've been all these years."

Aunt Maxi looked at me.

"I know all about my mom. I would love it if you two could put your differences aside and work this out so we can be a family."

"Fine. How about Buzz In and Out around noon?" Aunt Maxi asked.

There was a knock at the door. I stuck my head out the swinging door and noticed it was Big Bib.

"Perfect." Mom's eyes squinted when she smiled. Relief washed all over me as I headed to the door to let him in.

CHAPTER ELEVEN

"How many apple crisps do we have left?" I asked Bunny on my way over to make more coffee at the coffee bar.

"Just a few. Why?" she asked and handed a customer back some change from the register.

"I'm going to take them to Fred's wife." Spencer had told me she was back in town from visiting her sister.

"How many pup-sicles do we have left? I got a call asking if you could sell them in the size of the small ice bags that people buy for their coolers." She opened the glass case and started to combine some of the pastries to make room for the ones we'd just baked to put out.

"I can do that." I noted that I was going to probably use the last two watermelons and I could buy more from Hill's Orchard when I took the apple crisps out there. "When do they need them?"

"I told them I'd call them back," she called from the tea station where she was refilling the sugar jar.

After making a batch of pup-sicles to freeze so the customer could pick them up this afternoon, I got some of the pastries started in anticipation of the weekend, after I went to visit with Fred's widow, I'd get those baked and ready to freeze.

Bunny had everything covered. The boardwalk traffic had died down and the lake traffic had picked up. Pepper and I walked down to Crooked Cat.

"Hey," Leslie waved from a chair that was one of many in a circle. "Excuse me." She got up and put the book that was in her hands on her seat. "I'm sorry you couldn't make it last night. Crissy is really fun."

She bent down to pat Pepper.

"Oh good. I'm so glad you two got together. Next time." I promised. "Did I interrupt?"

"Book club meeting. We have it here once a month on Wednesday afternoons." She pointed to a sign that was posted by the register. "It's open to the public."

I eyed the group of women to see which one was Ida Combs.

"It's only an hour because most of the women work and come on their lunch break. What's up?" she asked.

My phone chirped in my back pocket. I sent it to voicemail when I saw it was Jeremy. He was probably calling about Tank and if there were any potential adoptive parents. I'd call him back.

"I'm not sure if you heard that Fred Hill was murdered." It was sort of a touchy subject with Leslie's mom being murdered, but I needed to find out some information.

"Crissy told me that you found him like you did my mama." She had an eek look on her face.

"Yeah." I frowned. "I'm here because I'm going to be looking into the case as Louise Carlton's lawyer."

"How can I help?" she asked.

"I need any and all information you might have on Ayam Cemani, a type of exotic chicken." I wasn't even sure if I was pronouncing it right.

"I've never heard of that before, but Joanne Stone is here and she's Honey Springs's librarian." Leslie put her hand in the air and waved it calling over to the group, "Joanne, can you come here for a minute?"

A woman with her long red hair braided in two nodded and came over. She was fairly young. Small orange freckles dotted all over her face.

"Hi," she said in a chipper voice.

"Hi," I smiled back.

With a quick introduction, I was pleased to know that she'd been in the coffeehouse before.

"Let me go look around and see what I might have while you two talk." Leslie excused herself.

"I have a lot of information on different species of chickens. I'm sure there's something on the Ayam Cemani. Why don't I gather some information when I get back to the library and I'll drop it off to the coffeehouse." She was very helpful.

"You don't mind?" I asked knowing that I'd have to pedal to town to the library.

"Not at all." It was so nice and refreshing to be around a town where everyone looked out for each other.

"When you do stop by, coffee and pastry on me." I grabbed a piece of paper from Leslie's counter and quickly wrote down my phone number and gave it to her.

She made her way back to the book club.

"I don't know who on earth has this type of chicken." Leslie brought back an encyclopedia with a photo of a black chicken. "But these animals are called the Lamborghini of chickens."

"Huh?" I drew back, my brows furrowed.

I followed her finger as she leaned toward me to read along.

"It says here that these birds are very rare and can sell for over twenty-five hundred dollars," she read what I'd already learned from my own internet search.

But hearing someone else say it out loud only made me gnaw on the thought that I might be right. . . .someone else had motive to kill Fred.

"What did Joanne say?" she asked.

"She's going to get some information together for me and bring it by the coffeehouse." I looked over at the group. "I'm in a hurry, but can you point out Ida Combs to me?"

"Sure. She's the one over there with that big brown bun on top of her head and cat-eye rhinestone glasses."

I took a mental picture in my head so when I did go to the courthouse to check out a few things, that I'd remember her.

"Thanks, Leslie. You're the best." I patted my leg for Pepper to come. "Come down for a treat on me."

CHAPTER TWELVE

"Hello there, Roxy," Spencer answered his phone.

"Good afternoon. What do you think about Bertie?" I asked and wondered if he'd thought she'd be a good motive for Fred's death.

I took Pepper and a The Bean Hive to-go bag with the honey apple crisps for Jean Hill out of the bike basket and unclipped the small cooler I'd strapped on the back of my bike filled with some pup-sicles. I wasn't sure what type of animals Fred had, but I knew if he did have some other than Bertie, they'd enjoy a treat on a warm day.

Pepper scurried up the steps of the cabin. I wedged my phone between my ear and shoulder so I could unlock the door.

"Who is Bertie?" Spencer asked.

"The chicken Fred Hill adopted from Pet Palace. The one with the expensive eggs." I changed Pepper's water and grabbed my car keys. Pepper was going to stay home while I ran my errand to see Jean Hill and dropped by the courthouse to check on my license. I continued, "Don't you know what this means?"

"I might have an idea where you are going with this, but why don't you tell me." Spencer obviously found my updates more entertaining than informative.

Call waiting rang in and it was Jeremy again. I'd completely forgotten he'd called earlier.

"Someone wanted the chicken because they knew it was worth money." It sounded like a good idea.

"If that's the case, who? If someone wanted the chicken, they'd have taken it when they killed Fred. On the other hand, maybe it was a reason for Louise to get Bertie back after she found out how much the eggs sold for because Jean Hill told me that Pet Palace called to see if she wanted to give Bertie back so Louise could adopt her out again," he informed me. "I went to see Louise."

"She told me. She also asked me to be her lawyer," I said.

"Yeah. She said she was getting a lawyer but she didn't say it was you." There was some jibber jabber coming across his cop radio. "Listen, I appreciate all the information. This time you're off base. Let me know if you hear anything else."

"That didn't go well," I muttered after he hung up.

I had a few minutes to drive to Hill's Orchard so I decided to call Jeremy back. He'd not left a message so it probably wasn't urgent.

"Pet Palace. Are you ready to adopt your fur baby?" Jeremy answered with his standard greeting.

"Hi, Jeremy. I'm sorry I missed your call." My stomach growled.

The apple crisps smelled so good. Why was it that when I was stressed, I wanted to eat?

"Roxy, I'm so glad you called back. Louise has decided not to come into work and I can't run this place on my own. I need sleep." He sounded tired. "If you could just come around four and volunteer just for a few hours, I'd ever be so grateful. I'm taking some night classes at the community college and I really don't want to miss class."

"I. . ." I gnawed on the time I'd lose looking into things, and if I did go, I wouldn't have time to get to the courthouse and I really wanted to.

"You know I'd never ask you if I didn't truly need you. If Louise didn't need you." He had to throw in Louise, which sent me on a guilt trip.

"You know I will." It wasn't even an option.

"You're such a good friend," he said with more relief in his voice.

"What are friends for?" I was lucky to have found a group of friends in Honey Springs that I considered family. "I'll see you soon and I'll bring you a couple treats."

The high school gals would be at the coffeehouse to finish off the day by the time I left Hill's Orchard and made it back to the coffeehouse. I'd make sure they were good for the night and check in on Tank since he'd be back before I went to Pet Palace.

The gravel parking lot at Hill's Orchard was empty. An unusual sight for the middle of the week. Sad really. It was hard to imagine Fred in his usual John Deere attire not muddling around the orchard or the Farmer's Market showing me all the different crossbreeds of fruits he'd been working on. He was particularly proud of his grapple. His version of the combined grape and apple. They were a little too tart for the baking I liked to do and I passed on those, even though he continued to try to get me to try them.

"Roxy? Is that you?" Jean Hill called from the front porch of the small ranch home she and Fred shared.

"It is." I walked toward her with a The Bean Hive bag dangling from my fingers. "I wanted to bring you some apple honey crisps that were baked with the last batch of apples I'd gotten from Fred."

"Oh, Roxy. You're so thoughtful." Her face showed the sadness in her life. "Please come in."

"Are you sure?" I asked and handed her the bag.

"I'm positive. Fred adored you, though he could be a bit of a grump sometimes." There was a faint smile behind the dark bags, frown and unkempt hair. "It'll be good to have some company who likes to eat Fred's creations as much as I do. These will be so good with a cup of fresh coffee. Not that I could outdo The Bean Hive coffee, but I did just make a pot."

"Alright." I nodded and stepped inside of their house.

As many times as I've been to the orchard, I'd never been into their house. It was pretty much as I expected. A sixties ranch that was in serious need of an update. The carpet was orange, there was wallpaper on every wall and the kitchen had an old wooden table with scarred chairs butted up to it. The cushions on the chairs were the exact same pattern of the apple wallpaper, which I'm sure in the day was expensive to do. Something Jean probably wanted and Fred grumbled the entire time.

"Here you go." Jean set a steaming coffee cup with a picture of a chicken on it in front of me.

"Thank you." I looked around.

There was a beautiful pie cabinet that'd be great as a display case for the coffeehouse. Too bad it was here and not on the floor of Wild and Whimsy. She didn't use it as a pie cabinet. The doors were open and there were framed photos that detailed their life. Even a couple of trophies were on a shelf along with some journal type books. The laptop computer was on the bottom shelf with a basket that looked as though it held bills.

"Fred sure did love chickens." I pointed to the cup.

"Have you ever heard of someone adopting a chicken?" She offered a half smile. "Fred was so excited when he adopted Bertie."

"I had no idea he was selling eggs." It was my lead-in question and I was pretty proud of myself.

"He was just researching it." She shook her head.

"Really." I brought the coffee up to my mouth.

Jean pushed a plate with one of the apple crisps across the table.

"Those are for you." I shook my hand at it. "Where is Bertie?"

"She's in the fancy coop he made in our shed behind the house. All of his research is out there too. There is a strict schedule he kept to feed her." She looked at her watch. "Which is in about five minutes."

"I'll help when you're ready." It was perfect. I wanted to get a gander at this expensive bird.

"No. No," she insisted. "You've come to visit. I couldn't put you to work."

"I'm here to help you." I wished I was better at easing into something but I wasn't. It was the lawyer in me that was direct with questioning. "Do you know why anyone would want to kill Fred?"

"Officer Shepard asked me the same thing." She shook her head. The corners of her eyes dipped. "He'd even mentioned TJ Holmes, but as far as I knew, that was over and done with."

"I'd heard about that. Can you tell me what the court verdict was?" I asked.

"Fred said they'd come to an agreement and that was it. Fred didn't let me in on the business. He really enjoyed doing it so I just helped here and there like the Farmer's Market." She smiled at the fond memory. "We'd load up on Sunday night." She stopped. Her eyes widened and she looked at me. "You know," She studied my face. "There was someone who stopped by late Sunday night after we'd packed up the truck with the market goodies. Fred seemed really fidgety when he came back in."

"Did he tell you who the visitor was?" I asked.

"No." She shook her head. "When we saw the headlights coming up the drive, Fred told me to go on in the house because my arthritis was acting up and I needed to rest." She rubbed her hand. "Sometimes doing the repetitive motion of putting the fruit in the wooden baskets got to my hands."

"What about that visitor?" I asked. "Did you get a look at them?"

"I don't even know if it was a man or a woman. They were dressed in black. They had on one of those sweatshirts all the kids are wearing with the hood up." She tsked. "Kids." She rolled her eyes. "Anyway, Fred figured it was someone who was traveling through town or a new summer citizen who saw our orchard sign out front. We get a lot of drive-by traffic and Fred always let them go into the shop and buy. So we just figured it was one of them. It was how Fred was acting that made me wonder who it was."

"He didn't tell you?" I asked.

"I asked and he said that it wasn't for me to worry." Her brows dipped. "Do you think that has something to do with the person who killed him?"

Worry set on her face.

"Now I wished I'd pressed him. Officer Shepard took all of Fred's work receipts and the sign-in journals, even his desktop computer. I don't know what on earth they're going to find. Honey, I have no idea how to use a computer."

"I forgot all about the sign-in journals." I recalled Fred always telling me to sign his book every time I came to visit.

"Oh yeah." She nodded with a simple smile. "He loved seeing all the different places people are from, especially the summer citizens. He took pride in them coming by every summer and stocking up on his labor. Just recently he started to make spreadsheets on his laptop."

"That's not your laptop?" I pointed to the pie chest.

"Heavens to Betsy, no." She shoved her hand toward me as if she were brushing off my observation. "Fred was always on that darn thing. Do you think I should've told Officer Shepard about it?"

"I'm more than happy to take it to him." *After I'm done looking through it,* I thought and hoped she'd agree.

"You'd do that? Roxy, you are a doll." She stood up. "If you'll excuse me, I need to go to the ladies room and then go feed Bertie."

"You go and I'll wait right here." I held my coffee cup up in the air. "I'll finish my delicious cup of coffee, and then I'll help with Bertie."

My palms were itching to get my hands on that laptop. When I heard the bathroom door shut, I got up to get the laptop because I was afraid she'd change her mind if I didn't already have it in my hands.

Sadness draped over me as I looked at the photos. There were several with Jean and there were a few of a happy young couple sitting in front of what looked to be the first of the orchard. I wondered how long they'd lived here. Fred had even gotten a key to the city. One of the trophies was a key and there was a framed photo of him with a police officer.

My heart quickened as I looked at the photo. I blinked. As if it were in slow motion, I reached out to pick up the frame and bring it closer to me. Surely my eyes were deceiving me.

"I guess I'll stay here. I'll have to hire someone for the orchard. I reckon' they're gonna have to haul me off one day like they did Fred. That realtor Doris Blankenship stopped by and left her card. She's a nosy one, that one. She insisted on taking a look around even though I told her I wasn't moving." I heard Jean talking, but it was muted because there was so much noise in my head about the photo with Patrick in it. "Roxy, are you okay?" Jean was suddenly standing next to me.

I hadn't even heard her come back into the kitchen. I blinked a couple of times to bring me back to the present.

"I'm. . ." I gulped to try and wet my dry mouth. "I had no idea Patrick Cane was a police officer."

"Isn't he handsome?" she asked. "Such a tragedy what happened, isn't it?"

My fingers gripped the frame so hard that they started to hurt.

"What happened?" I asked.

"I can't recall all of it." She took the frame from me and put it back in its place. "The drowning or something." She waved her hand. "Ready to go meet Bertie?"

"Yeah." It took all my energy to pick up the laptop. The lightweight computer suddenly felt like fifty pounds.

Mindlessly, I followed Jean out to the shed and the only thing that brought me out of my thoughts was her shriek.

"Bertie's gone! Someone's stolen Bertie!"

CHAPTER THIRTEEN

"*We* are going to have to stop meeting like this." Spencer nudged me. "I'm beginning to think that you aren't listening to me."

The chicken's shed was nicer than the cabin. It was swarmed by cops and detectives. Pictures were being taken, prints were being dusted, and Jean was crying in the corner.

"At least it's not a dead body," I muttered and tried to get the image of Patrick in a police uniform out of my head.

How did I not know? Why hadn't it come up? He was my fiancé. I felt for my ring.

"What were you doing here anyway?" he asked.

"I'd made apple honey crisps with the last batch of apples Fred had sold me. Like all us southern women, I was dropping some off for Jean. I knew she'd appreciate the fruits of her husband's labor in a pastry. He'd come in the coffeehouse and tell me how much she loved my sweets." I probably should've brought up the laptop, but I didn't.

After we'd discovered the lock on Bertie's cage had been cut in two, she ran into the house while I ran to my car with the laptop because I knew she was calling the police.

"We finished our coffee and came out here to feed Bertie. That's when she noticed the lock had been cut." I shrugged. "Did you know that Patrick was a police officer?"

"Of course, we didn't work together. He was out of it by the time I got here." His brows dipped. "Why? You think he can solve this?" he asked in a sarcastic manner that struck a chord with me.

"No. I was just asking." I didn't like his attitude. "I was just asking. When did you start working here?"

"Four years ago." He gave me a curious look. "What's this got to do with Bertie?"

"Nothing. I was just making small talk." So, four years ago Patrick wasn't on the force. Four years ago I thought I was happily married, but I knew different deep down.

"No time for small talk. If you don't have anything to add about Bertie, then you can go," he said.

"The only thing I know is that my egg and chicken theory might not be so far off the mark as a reason for someone to have killed Fred." The idea continued to noodle in my head. "Think about it. The killer found out that Bertie is a rare species that can bring upward to a few thousand dollars." I snapped my fingers. "Jean did tell me that someone stopped by late Sunday night after hours, which isn't uncommon, but Fred was very fidgety after he came back into the house."

He quickly flipped through his notebook. He looked at me.

"She didn't even mention that during her interview." He slid his eyes over to Jean who was still talking to the other officers.

"She told me. She also told me that you took Fred's computer. Did he have any emails about the bird?" I asked, wondering if there was a trail.

"There wasn't anything on there. He did his bookkeeping and that was it." He flipped his notebook shut. "If you'll excuse me. I'm going to go ask her about that mystery visitor."

"Yeah. No problem." I waved 'bye. "I've got to go to Pet Palace and do some extra volunteering."

Poor Bertie. My thoughts were focused on who took her on my drive over to Pet Palace. While I was at Pet Palace, I was going to find the paperwork on Bertie's adoption. Jean said that Fred had started to input the visitors' information in a spreadsheet on his laptop. I couldn't help but wonder if any of those visitors had an interest in fancy chickens.

Before I knew it, I'd already pulled up to Pet Palace. Emily was still at The Bean Hive when I called to check in on how the afternoon went. She said that she'd put more pastries in the refrigerator for overnight and had taken it upon herself to make more pup-sicles because once the customer took theirs down to the marina, The Bean Hive was flooded with orders.

"Also, a lady came in here looking for you. She said she was your mom," Emily said. "I mean you've never mentioned your mother, but she sure did look like you."

"Then it was my mom. Did she say what she wanted?" I asked and had completely forgotten about the lunch she'd had with Aunt Maxi.

"No, she said that she'd see you later." Emily was a natural and I was lucky to have her as an employee. "Also, I wanted to talk to you about Tank. Can I take him home again tonight? My sister is coming into town for the start of summer and she's been looking for a dog. I think he'd really like her."

And that's another thing I loved about Emily. She got animals like me. And her words when she said that she thought Tank would like her sister was so much better than saying her sister would like Tank. Ultimately it was our fur babies who made the decision to love us and when they did, it was unconditional.

"That'd be great. I hope they are a good match. He's a great dog." Jeremy peeked his head out the door and tapped his watch. "I've got to go."

"One more thing," Emily hesitated. "I wanted to know if there was a full-time position here for the summer?"

"Seriously?" I couldn't believe it. "That'd be great."

"Awesome. It'll help pay for school. I can start tomorrow." Her ambition was welcomed. "I can come anytime."

"Why don't you meet me there at four-thirty a.m." It wasn't like I needed the help so early in the morning, but it would be nice to show her the ropes in case I did need her to come. Not to mention whenever Patrick and I do get married, I'm going to have to have someone open the coffeehouse.

"That's wonderful." The excitement in her voice made me excited. "I'm so looking forward to learning from you."

The call waiting beeped in.

"Emily, I've got to run, I'll see you in the morning. And thank you so much for all you do." I always liked to hear praise when I was her age and I wanted to make sure she knew just how much I did appreciate her. I clicked over. "Hey," I greeted Patrick. "I was about to call you in a few minutes."

"I don't know how you did it, but it seems like your mom and Maxi were actually laughing together today." His words were music to my ears.

"Really?" I asked and noticed Jeremy was still staring at me.

"Yeah, I had to go to Buzz In and Out to fix a bad electrical outlet and there they were, sharing a big piece of mud pie." He laughed.

"I'm shocked." My mouth dropped open. Never in a million years did I ever think they'd sit down together, much less share a piece of pie. "But delighted."

"It was a good sight to see, especially remembering how you used to talk about your mom when you'd come visit." His voice was so comforting. "Do you want to grab some supper?"

"I wish I could but I'm actually sitting in the parking lot of Pet Palace with Jeremy giving me the stare down. He needs a volunteer so he can go to his summer class. Rain check?" I asked.

I did want to ask him about that whole cop thing, but there wasn't enough time right now. It all went back to me not really knowing him and him not really knowing me, not that there was much to know.

"I'll bring something to you," he suggested.

"Perfect. Text me when you are here because I'm going to lock the door and do you mind swinging by the house and grabbing Pepper?" Pepper loved to come see his friends at Pet Palace.

Jeremy was standing by the car door and tapping his foot. I grabbed the laptop and the cooler. Since I didn't see any animals at Hill's Orchard, I knew these animals would gobble them up.

"I've got to run." He touched my shoulder. "Tag you're it."

"No problem. But. . ." I had a few questions.

"What?" He looked down his nose at me.

"What's going on with Louise?" I asked.

"She's upset and trying to get things in order if she does end up going to jail." He shrugged.

"What things?" I was curious. "As her lawyer, I'd like to know these things."

"Wait." He gave me a curious look. "You're her lawyer?"

"She asked me to be and I've got to make sure the paperwork is all completed, but yeah, I'm doing a little snooping." I hugged the laptop with one hand and I'd gripped the cooler with the pup-sicles in the other.

"Hopefully you can help her like you did in the last investigation." He smiled. "Do you have any information?"

"Just that the darn chicken y'all let Fred adopt is worth a mint."

"Huh?" His nose curled like I was stink talking. "A chicken?"

"Yes. Something about being a rare bird and Louise told me the eggs from it can sell upwards of three hundred dollars." It sounded so ridiculous coming out of my mouth. "I even have Joanne pulling me some articles on the darn bird at the library."

"Were they why he and Louise were fighting?" he asked.

"You know about that?" I asked.

"Know about it?" He took a step back. "He was crazy over some eggs and I wasn't sure what he was talking about. But Louise said he wasn't getting them. He told her that by all rights they were his eggs and he'd fight her until he died."

My eyes popped open. I gulped.

"That's the same look Officer Shepard gave me when I told him about it." Jeremy shuffled toward his car with his keys in his hand. "I'd love to sit here and chit-chat, but I've got to get to class. Even more important now than before. If you can't help Louise, it looks like I'll be looking for another job." He stopped shy of his car. "By the way, I left all the poop cleanup for you." He winked and jumped into his car.

I tucked my bottom lip into my teeth. I'd wished Jeremy hadn't told Spencer that about Louise and Fred. Now Louise looked guiltier than ever.

CHAPTER FOURTEEN

Thankfully Jeremy had left the lights on for me. Pet Palace closed at five o'clock p.m. It was really a perfect time. The animals needed to be fed, the cages cleaned again, the animals needed to be let out and tucked in for bed. By the time all of the chores were completed, it was almost nine p.m. and that was with two volunteers.

"Hi, Louise," I called my friend once I locked the door behind me. And stuck a few of the pup-sicles in the freezer that was right inside the lobby where Louise stored homemade kibble for purchase. "How's it going?"

"Oh, you know." She sniffled on the other end of the line. "I just can't believe I'm the only suspect."

"I'm not so sure that's the truth." I walked around the counter in the front lobby of Pet Palace and set the laptop down. After I finished cleaning the cats, I figured I could sit up here and wait for Patrick to come with our supper. Plus, it would give me some time to go through some of the laptop.

"What? Who?" she asked.

"Did anyone ever come to you about a rare chicken like Bertie? Because she's been stolen from her pen at Hill's Orchard." Though she gasped on the other end of the phone, I still talked. "Someone knew about the chicken and wanted it. Not only that, but Jean said someone had come by the orchard late at night on Sunday. She said that Fred fidgeted all night long."

"Did she say who it was?" she asked. There was a bit of hope in her voice.

"No, but I also got another tip that I need to explore tomorrow." Even though I hadn't checked on the status of my law licenses, I was going ahead like I was putting together a case. "Remember, anything I tell you is only between me and you."

A dog barked from the dog kennel side of Pet Palace that sparked the entire dog population to hoot and howl.

"What's going on there?" Louise asked. "Is something wrong? They don't do that unless they hear something."

"That doesn't make me feel good." I walked over to the hall that led to the dogs.

I thought I heard something like the rattle of a chain, but the dogs were so loud that I couldn't make it out. Suddenly, they stopped. All at once. Goosebumps crawled up my legs, my body and stopped on my neck.

"They stopped." I told Louise hoping she'd tell me that everything was okay. I walked back to the front door and didn't see any cars. I brushed it off as an active imagination for the pure fact that I was talking to Louise about a murder and my scare meter had already been turned on high.

"You be careful out there." Her words didn't make my nerves ease up.

Pet Palace was out there. It was in the rural area of Honey Springs. There was enough land that there could be an add-on. And it was prime real estate.

"Real estate," I whispered.

"What?" Louise called from the other end of the phone.

"Nothing. Listen, no matter what I tell you, you can't tell anyone. If you tell anyone and Spencer hears what I'm doing, it could hinder your case and then you'd really go to jail." I had to get off the phone.

There was limited time to clean the cages and get right to the laptop.

"Why don't you come by the coffeehouse late morning and we'll get a strategy." After she agreed, I flipped the phone shut and stuck it in my pocket to wait for Patrick to text me so I could let him in.

I had a system when I volunteered at Pet Palace. The cats always needed a litter change and the smell was so much better after they were cleaned. That was the first thing I did after I put a pup-sicle in each one of their water bowls. If they were low on kibble, I was sure to fill it to the brim. Not to mention I kicked a couple play mouse toys or balls that sent the sweet cats into a batting tizzy.

"Pepper!" My sweet Schnauzer rushed back to the cat side of Pet Palace.

He jumped up and down on me until I bent down to give him some rubbing. The cats in the area weren't too fazed by him. He'd lived there for a while before I'd adopted him and from what Louise had told me, Pepper had belonged to a man in the military who had to give Pepper up due to another tour of duty.

He was a bit of a yip-yapper and very active so he wasn't easily adoptable, but I truly believe he was meant for me. He was the perfect companion to keep me safe at night and a wonderful cheerleader for the coffeehouse. Louise knew he was a great dog and she'd let him walk around with her during the day while she cleaned. The other animals knew him and that was what made him so great to be around the animals that Louise brought in for me to help find a home at the coffeehouse.

"There you are." Patrick was out of breath when he rounded the corner of the cat kennels. Sassy was with him. She moseyed up to me, sniffed me and sat down. "Pepper took off like a jet and he sniffed you out."

"Hi." I stood up with a pair of yellow gloves on and a big black trash bag of cat litter in one hand. I leaned over really far and gave him a kiss. "How was your day?"

"I'll tell you over Chinese." He pointed behind him. "I've got it sitting on the front counter."

"Wait." My brows furrowed. "How did you get in?"

"The front door was open." He looked at me under hooded brows. "You did tell me to text you."

I dropped the bag and ran out of the cat kennel with everyone on my heels.

"I didn't unlock that door," I called out over my shoulder.

The ruffle of papers and footsteps came from the front of the lobby. Patrick obviously heard me and shoved me out of the way, running around me.

"Stop there!" he screamed right as the person tried to get out of the door.

"The laptop!" I screamed. "Get the laptop!"

The door stuck, the person dropped the laptop and pushed on the door, flinging it open and ran out.

"Did you get a good look?" My chest heaved up and down. I bent over to catch my breath.

Pepper jumped up and down like we were playing.

"No. They had on a pair of black jeans and a black hoodie that was pulled tight around the face and tied." He picked up the laptop and handed it to me.

"Black jeans and hoodie." My stomach dropped. My eyes did a slow slide to lock gazes with him. "Jean Hill said the late night visitor had on black and a hooded sweatshirt."

"What's on that computer?" he asked.

"Jean let me take it because there might be a clue on there about the visitor. She said that Fred had been logging in all the visitors from the written log. Spencer took the written logs from the shop and the desktop computer, but he didn't get this." I wagged it in the air at him.

"You need to turn that into the police," Patrick noted.

"No." I hugged it close to me. "What are you doing?" I asked when he started tapping away on his phone.

"I'm calling the police about the intruder." He stopped and looked at me.

"Oh no." I reached out to take it. He jerked it back. "Why didn't you tell me that you were a cop?"

"It doesn't matter. It's in the past." His brows dipped.

"This is exactly what I was saying the other day about how we didn't really know each other. I think as your future wife, this should've come up." It was a great way to get off the topic of the intruder and the laptop.

"We were separated for ten years. There's a lot of stuff that happened in ten years, but my love for you never stopped. When I saw you on the boardwalk that morning with the coffee and treats for my crew, I went right back to being head over heels in love with you." He always knew what to say to make my heart melt.

When I'd come back to Honey Springs, it wasn't until the weekend that The Bean Hive opened that I ran into him. He and his construction crew were working so hard to finish for the grand opening of the newly revitalized boardwalk. I'd watched them day in and day out. They even got there as early as I did. I felt bad for them, so I took them donuts and coffee, never once realizing it was Patrick underneath that hard hat.

"To make up for it, you can help me go through the laptop and help me use your resources to get Louise off the hook." I grinned.

"Fine. But," he held up a finger, "I'm calling Spencer right now to come here and look around. You can put the laptop in your car."

"He's going to ask questions." I didn't want to lie about the intruder having the laptop. "I can't lie. I'm trying to get some more clues to get Louise off the hook."

"Louise has a key to the place." He made a good point.

"So does every other volunteer." I gulped. "I think the intruder was here before I got here." I was thankful I didn't walk in here and find Jeremy dead. "I called Louise when I got here and the dogs started to go nuts and bark. She said they didn't do that unless there was something wrong."

"Did you look in the dog kennel?" he asked.

"No." I shook my head. "They suddenly stopped and I just figured one started barking and the others followed suit."

"That's it." Patrick had heard enough. "I'm calling Spencer."

While we waited for the Spencer to show up, we munched on some crab Rangoon and some spring rolls. We decided not to go back in the dog kennel in case the intruder was waiting in there and we didn't want to mess up any fingerprints or evidence.

"See," I told Spencer when he arrived and offered him a spring roll, "Louise wasn't here when the intruder came. You can check my phone records."

"I believe you. And I'm not saying you're right, but someone is going to great lengths to make it seem like she killed Fred," he noted.

"A little too much if you ask me," Patrick stated.

"I didn't ask you." Spencer glanced up at Patrick.

"When it comes to the safety of my fiancée," Patrick put his arm around me, "then it becomes my business."

"You need to tell your fiancée to stop snooping around." He pointed to me. "This is the third time in the matter of a twenty-four hour period that I've told her to stay away."

"You know I can't do that when I'm Louise's lawyer. I'm looking for clues just like you are and I think I've proven my case that a similarly dressed person showed up at Fred's and now showed up here tonight. It wasn't Louise Carlton." I knew I had him.

"What on earth is going on?" Jeremy walked in through the front door. His backpack slung over his shoulder.

"There was an intruder. They must've been hiding out in the dog kennel while you were here," I choked out.

Tears started to form on my eyes. The thought of me being there with a killer suddenly hit me.

Jeremy ran his hands through his hair. "Oh my God. Did you catch 'em?" he asked Spencer.

"No, they got away." Spencer delivered the bad news right as Louise hurried through the door.

"Louise, where are the eggs that Fred wanted?" I asked, wondering if the intruder was looking for the eggs.

"They are at my home. Safe and sound," Louise noted. "Are the dogs okay?" There was a worried look in her eyes.

"They seemed fine, but I'm not much of a dog person so I don't know." Spencer's words met dead silence.

Patrick's lips grew into a big ole smile. He looked at me and I snarled at Spencer. I never trust a person who doesn't love dogs.

CHAPTER FIFTEEN

"Okay." Patrick opened the laptop. "Let's take a look at this visitor's log Jean told you about."

Patrick sat at one of the café tables in the coffeehouse and Mom made the lavender coffee that I've been dying to have since this morning while I busied myself with grabbing ingredients to make southern pound cake. It was a nice light dessert that would pair well with Mom's lavender coffee. I'd decided it was going to be tomorrow's special.

Pepper and Sassy had gotten a treat from Mom and now shared Pepper's big pillow. Pepper was curled up in a ball while Sassy was on her back with her legs in the air. Both of their eyes were closed tight.

After Spencer let Patrick and I leave, I'd called Mom to meet us at the coffeehouse. Even though Emily had said she had everything covered, I wanted to pick up the packet Joanne had left for me about the fancy chicken, and I wanted to bake. My mind needed to relax and it was the only way I knew how.

I'd also told Louise there was no need to come meet me at the coffeehouse in the morning because there was sufficient evidence that there was another suspect. Spencer had even confirmed that the person in the black outfit was now the main person of interest. Especially since they'd broken into Pet Palace.

Patrick eased back in the chair and stared at the screen.

"What?" I asked with a handful of ingredients in my arms as I pushed through the swinging door between the kitchen and the coffee-house. I put them on the counter and walked up behind him.

There was a security box that'd popped up. The background photo was of Bertie.

"Bertie," I let out an exhausted sigh. "I completely forgot to get on the computer and pull her adoption papers Fred would've had to fill out."

"If I can get into his computer, I can sorta hack into the Pet Palace computer," he said nonchalantly.

"Are you serious?" My mouth dropped open.

"I was in the internet crime division of the department after I stepped down from being in the field." He was starting to open up about that part of his life now that I knew about it.

Though I wanted to know the truth behind the drowning Jean had mentioned, I didn't want to press him. Like he said, it was in the past and it didn't define our relationship. It still didn't keep me from wanting to know everything about him and his past.

"Don't look at me that way." He glanced over his shoulder and looked at me.

"You mean all the time I was trying to figure out what happened to Alexis Roarke, you could've helped me?" I asked.

"That's the police's job, not mine." He turned back around. "Apples," he said and typed at the same time.

The laptop screen blinked, letting us know apple wasn't the password.

"Bertie," I suggested.

He typed in Bertie and hit the okay button. The laptop screen blinked again.

"It can't be too hard. One thing I learned in the hack division is that most passwords are so simple that whoever is trying to break in puts in too much thought." He clicked away on the keyboard a few times.

The screen blinked back at him a few times.

I walked back to the counter. In the electric mixing bowl I combined the butter and sugar. While the electric mixer made the two ingredients fluffy, I pulled the envelope Joanne had left for me from the side of the register where Emily had left it.

"Ayam Cemani," I read the front of the envelope. "Try typing in 'Ayam Cemani'."

"Spell it for me." Patrick's fingers were ready to type.

"A-y-a-m-c-e-m-a-n-i." I sucked in a deep breath hoping that it was complicated enough for anyone who tried to get into Fred's computer but easy enough for him.

"Voila!" Patrick smacked his hands together and vigorously rubbed them. He set them back on the screen. "Now let's look at his history."

It sounded like a good place to start. I let him do his investigating while I continued to make the pound cake.

"It looks like he's been investigating exactly how to sell the eggs. There doesn't seem to be many websites devoted to it because it looks like these types of birds come from Asia and it's illegal to ship them." He continued to read articles he was coming across. "But they can be put in Asian meat markets in the United States. The meat is very sought out. It looks like Fred's been looking up Asian markets across the states."

"If that's the case," I added the flour and milk, alternating each one into the mixing bowl while the paddle was going round and round, "then he was probably planning to sell Bertie's eggs."

"It also looks like he's been investigating this for about eight days. Not long." Patrick continued to scroll through. "I'm going to jump into his email."

"That's a great idea to see if he reached out to any of the markets and then we can call them." It sounded like a good plan and I'd seen people on TV do things like this.

Slowing down the speed of the mixer, I added in the extracts. The warm smell of vanilla swirled up from the bowl. It was such a comforting smell.

"Try this." Mom held a cup of coffee underneath my nose. The lavender mixed with the vanilla. "It's decaffeinated."

"Oh, I'll get the pound cakes in the oven and we can enjoy a bite." I wiggled my brows and scooped all the batter into a few of the pound cake molds before heading back to the kitchen and sticking them in the preheated oven.

While I waited for the timer to go off, Mom sat down with Patrick at the table. I used the time to wipe off one of the chalkboards that was hanging on the wall with the specials on it. In fancy calligraphy, I wrote tomorrow's daily special and joined Mom and Patrick.

Patrick clicked away. His eyes scanned down the screen quickly before he'd click again.

"Tell me about you and Aunt Maxi." It was the first time I'd asked her about it.

"She accepted the reasons I didn't want you to come to Honey Springs and I realized that I probably should've come a few days and that it wouldn't've killed me. I think we both realized we have been selfish with how much we love you." She reached over and squeezed my hand. "We only want the best for you. I agree with her that you belong here in Honey Springs. There's nothing stopping me from staying here."

"Do you have plans?" I asked.

"You know that I met with that realtor, Doris. I also enjoyed putting up the new banners along the carriage lights on the boardwalk and in town. So right now, I think I just want to volunteer and find a house." She smiled. "Get my stuff out of your hair."

"Look here." Patrick smacked his hands together.

Sassy and Pepper jumped up. The clap of Patrick's hands startled them. They started to bark. Mom got up and patted them to settle them down.

"He's gotten a couple of markets interested in purchasing Bertie's eggs for three hundred a pop. But here's the kicker." He pointed to an email that was to Honey Springs National Bank. "He had an appointment tomorrow to discuss taking out a second mortgage on the property. With a quick search of the property valuation, it could be sold for one point four million dollars. If it's foreclosed, Jean would get nothing. If it's sold, the seller will make a mint."

"You know, Doris said something about how she gets information from the bank about upcoming foreclosures. She's got an in, she said. And that there was a small ranch on an orchard coming up for sale that she was looking at purchasing. Not the orchard, but a small ranch that would fit my needs," Mom said. "You don't think she was talking about Hill's Orchard, do you?"

A recollection of Jean coming down her hall and talking to me as I stood at the pie cabinet looking at the photo of Fred and Patrick together during the key to Honey Springs ceremony.

"Jean told me that Doris had stopped by and insisted on looking around the house even though Jean told her she wasn't moving. I'll bet Doris knew about the foreclosure and with Fred out of the way. . ." I didn't dare say it. "Only one way to find out. Go see Doris." My brows rose. "Aunt Maxi mentioned that Doris had sold TJ Holmes the property and she was the one who told him to get the property line inspected."

"I hate to say it, but Doris did just come into a lump sum of money from an uncle who only had her as a niece. She called the office looking for property to use as a summer rental for a good tax write off. But if she can get the orchard," his voice faded off. "According to this email from the IRS a couple of days ago, it looks like he'd not been paying taxes or enough taxes on the orchard."

"So do you think that's why he's taking out a second mortgage?" I wondered. "I couldn't imagine it's a foreclosure. All Jean would have to do is follow through with getting a second mortgage to pay off the house."

"But what would be her income?" Mom asked.

"She said something about hiring people to work at the orchard." I shrugged. "Or TJ would definitely take over his part of the land."

"Then TJ. He could be in on it with Doris if they're both trying to get a hand in the money pot." Patrick threw it out there. "Of course, this is all just thinking out loud."

"And most of it really doesn't make sense." I pretended like it didn't, but it made perfect sense for TJ and Doris to be on the top of the suspect list.

"TJ." Mom looked out into the coffeehouse as if she were trying to remember something. "There was a TJ that called Doris while we were looking at a townhouse in town. She said that she was closer than ever on the property. Is that a clue?"

I jumped up and grabbed one of the sawhorse chalkboards we used to put on the boardwalk outside.

"We can do it like the TV detectives." I got excited and started writing suspect with a line under it and motive next to it. "There's a connection between them."

"The real world does it too." Patrick smiled.

"Oh yeah, I'm going to have to get used to the fact that you were once a cop." I glared at him before I gave him a kiss. "I like it much better that you're in construction now."

Mom stood with a big smile on her face. It was actually nice having her here for this part of my life. The first time I got married, she wasn't involved with us at all. She never got to know my ex-husband and I was grateful for that now. The timer in the kitchen dinged. Mom went in there and took the pound cakes out of the oven.

"So we can put Louise Carlton up here, but cross her out. I also think we need to put TJ Holmes on here because he had taken Fred to court over the land. According to him and Jean, the lawsuit has been settled." I wrote down bullet points under his name with key words. "Also Doris Blankenship can go on our list because she encouraged TJ to get the survey and could stand to gain a lot of money from the foreclosure if she was planning on doing something with the rest of the orchard." I tapped the chalkboard under TJ's name. "We can't forget that TJ also lied to Spencer about being at the marina at the time Fred was murdered."

"We don't know where he was during that time do we?" Patrick asked.

"No." I looked at my pitiful board. "I don't even think Jean knew about the foreclosure because she said she guessed she'd stay there until they packed her off too."

"I can make a pretend service call to TJ's house." Patrick was getting tricky and I liked it.

"Now you're acting like my fiancé." I bent down and gave him a kiss to remember.

Sassy and Pepper barked with delight.

CHAPTER SIXTEEN

*T*he next morning I decided to drive the car instead of my bike into town. I knew once I got Emily and Bunny settled, I'd show up at Doris's real estate office and see what she knew.

Patrick said he was going to check out TJ and Mom was going to go find a job that might suit her.

"That's all there is to opening?" Emily seemed pretty confident. She had her blond hair pulled back into a low ponytail and a The Bean Hive apron tied around her waist. "Nothing more?" she asked, making sure.

"That's it." I couldn't have been more pleased with her ability to catch on quickly.

She was there when Pepper and I had arrived. When we walked in and after I flipped on the lights, she'd already headed back to the kitchen to preheat the ovens and get the regular pastries out of the refrigerator.

"I noticed every morning you have your general pastries that please everyone." She pointed to the honey-glazed donuts as well as all the other flavors: the coffee soufflé, variety of scones, and of course the muffins and bagels. "Then you have your casserole or the lunch item of the day."

It was a simple concept really. The Bean Hive was a coffeehouse, not a diner or café. I specialized in any sort of coffee and tea you'd want. I also knew that people bonded over food, so the small variety of items kept my baking skills fresh. Also I made one lunch item a day that appealed to the customer who didn't particularly care for desserts as much as I did. I shudder at the thought of not loving baked goods, but everyone was different and I aimed to please.

Today's special was going to be the mini Kentucky hot brown again, only for the fact that I'd been spending the better part of the last couple of days trying to find suspects other than Louise. Now that she was no longer under the microscope, I felt like I could breathe easier, but my curiosity still had me craving to figure out exactly if TJ or Doris did it.

"As the morning goes on, I'll check the coffee and tea bar. Make sure the thermoses are filled and the condiments are stocked. I'll pick up trash, let Pepper out." Her jaw dropped. "Before I forget, my sister and Tank." She put her hands together. "Match made in heaven. She's going to stop by Pet Palace today and sign the adoption papers."

"Oh good." I felt a bit relieved knowing that Louise was going to be there to do it. She'd been so much happier since she'd been cleared off the suspect list. . .sort of. "He's such a sweet dog." I gave her arm a squeeze. "Today after Bunny gets here," I took out some of the velvet crunchies from the oven and replaced them with some more honey-glazed donuts. "I need to run into town."

"No problem. I'm more than happy to help wherever you need me." She pushed through the kitchen door with the crunchies in her hand. Without even looking, I knew she was going to put them in one of the doomed platters. Customers couldn't resist the gooey red velvet chocolate chip cookies.

By the time I cleaned up the kitchen and got most of the food ready for restocking while I was out, Aunt Maxi and Bunny Bowowski walked through the front door of the coffeehouse, flipping the sign to open for me.

"Here you go." I pushed a couple of hot coffees across the counter toward them.

"Hi, Emily." Bunny gave Emily a hug. "You're here early."

"Emily is going to be working more hours for me. Isn't that great?" We all liked Emily.

"I do love that you are here, but I'm going to miss you down at Honey Springs National." Aunt Maxi's mouth dipped down.

"Honey Springs National?" That was the bank Fred Hill had the appointment with today.

"My dad is the loan officer there and for the past few summers I've filled in as a teller when the employees go on summer vacations." It was strange to hear of the real citizens of Honey Springs going on vacation when we had a beautiful lake right in front of us. "I'm going to miss seeing everyone too, but I hope to go to baking school in the fall."

"You are?" I questioned.

"Yes, but my parents don't really want me to." She shrugged. "They want me to get a four-year degree and go into finance so I can take over my dad's job."

"Maybe I can stop by and have a talk with him," I suggested.

About what was Fred Hill, not so much about baking, though I would throw in some good stuff for good measure. Emily was wise beyond her years and I'm sure she knew what and how to get what she wanted. I just really wanted a reason to get in front of her father to ask a few questions. For Louise's case of course.

"Would you really? I'd be so grateful. There's not a bakery in town anymore and not that I want to hone in on your baking, but it is a need in the area." She had a point.

"I agree. I don't bake cakes or fancy desserts. Honey Springs does need a bakery." If you considered the baking section at our local Piggly Wiggly as a bakery, then have at it, but there wasn't a true shop just for baking. "Then it's settled. In a few minutes, I'll be off to run my errands."

"I do have to confess something." Emily had an *oh no* look on her face. "Last night when we had some down time, I got out your apple crisp recipe because I noticed we were practically out." She sucked in a breath as if she were trying to get her courage up.

"Go on," I encouraged her.

"I took it upon myself to make some." Her chin dropped to her chest.

"That's wonderful!" I was excited to see that she took it upon herself to make some more because I'd just grab things already made from the freezer until it was Sunday, the day I spent in the kitchen baking since the coffeehouse was closed half of the day.

It was closed because I needed at least that time to plan for the upcoming week.

"Are you sure?" She lifted her eyes toward me but kept her head down.

"Absolutely. Now don't cross my coffee creations." I winked. "Listen, when you are here, feel free to bake. I'm not a baker. I know that it seems like I know what I'm doing when it comes to the food side, but I don't. I make what I like and I make recipes that I know." I pointed to her. "You. You are a creator of ingredients. You are a go-getter and I find it very refreshing and much welcomed."

Emily threw her arms around me.

"Thank you, Roxy." She squeezed and I squeezed back.

"Good morning!" Mom called and entered the coffeehouse. "Are you ready?" she asked Aunt Maxi.

"What are you two up to?" I asked.

"One of my rentals is empty and I thought I'd let your mom look it. It's perfect for a single person. Right in town. A small yard." Aunt Maxi lifted her hands. "What more could you ask for?"

"You're going to sell it?" I asked.

Aunt Maxi really enjoyed visiting with her tenants.

"One won't kill me. Besides, I'm getting older. Not Bunny old." She just couldn't resist.

"You're catching up fast," Bunny quipped back. "Maxine Bloom, Floyd told me last night that you were down at the Moose shimmying and shaking your backside toward him." Bunny's lips pursed. "I wasn't going to say nothing, because Floyd told me, but now that you're insulting me."

I stepped between them.

"And we were doing so good the last few days." My brows drew together.

It was no secret that Bunny and Aunt Maxi weren't the best of friends, but she'd put up with Bunny for me. I'm sure she was doing the same thing with my mom.

"I can't get along with everyone you want me to." Aunt Maxi cocked a brow. "Come on." She pinched my mother on the arm. "Let's get out of here before I say something that's gonna make Roxy upset."

"Ouch." Mom rubbed it out and gave Aunt Maxi a cross look. "What's wrong with you?"

Aunt Maxi slid her gaze to Bunny.

"You'd argue with a fence post." Bunny waddled over to the coat rack and took the brown pocketbook from the crook of her arm. She replaced a The Bean Hive apron on the rack with her purse.

Before Aunt Maxi could protest, customers started to file into the coffeehouse. It was time to get on with everyone's day, including my agenda, which was to call the Asian markets Fred had contact with. Last night, Patrick had Googled the markets and got their contact information.

The first on my list was Happy Asian Market. Two of the four markets were in neighboring larger Kentucky cities while the other two were in Ohio, which wasn't but a couple of hours away. Much easier to transport eggs to and the only ones who'd responded to his request.

"Good morning," I greeted the person who answered the phone. "My name is Roxy and I live in Honey Springs, Kentucky. I'm calling on behalf of Fred Hill about the Ayam Cemani eggs."

"Oh yes. This is Angela, the market's buyer." It was a friendly lady. "Has he made a decision yet? I know we offered a very good exclusive deal."

"That's why I'm calling. He seemed to misplace the numbers you gave him. His memory isn't the best. Do you mind going over them with me again? We are going to be making the decision very soon." I grabbed a pen to write the information next to her contact information we'd written down last night.

"Sure. Let me grab it. Hold on." There was a short pause before she came back. "Did you say you were in Honey Springs because Fred wouldn't give us any information?"

This immediately took Asian Market and Angela off the list of potential suspects who could've taken Bertie.

"He's very private." I left it at that. "What were the numbers again?" I still wanted to find out.

"We are going to offer two hundred per egg. We know they are worth twice that but we have to have a profit too. We will come and pick them up from the orchard every six months. And it's exclusive."

"Thanks, Angela. I'll be in touch soon." I quickly clicked off before she could say another word.

I texted Patrick to let him know about Asian Market and to cross them off the list.

It was prime morning coffee time. The blenders were buzzing. Emily was making all the specialty coffees while Bunny took the orders and rang up the customers. I grabbed the envelope Joanne had left and wanted to see what else I could learn about the chicken before I called Saigon Market, the next Asian market on the list.

Interestingly enough, the Ayam Cemani was the most sought after chicken. They were all black including their organs. Some people believed magical powers come with the chicken because of the all black, which made them even more of a hot commodity. Joanne had circled different articles she'd copied that showed the differences in the cost of the eggs. The range was between two hundred and five hundred dollars. The chicken lays twenty to sixty eggs every three to six months. No wonder the Asian Market wanted exclusivity. They could charge whatever they wanted and monopolize the market around the area.

"Hi," I greeted the man who answered the phone at the Saigon Market. "This is Roxy Bloom, Fred Hill's assistant. I'm calling about the email concerning the Ayam Cemani eggs."

It was clear that the markets probably didn't want the chicken. They wanted the eggs. At even two hundred dollars a pop, Fred could easily pay the back taxes he owed the IRS.

"Aw, yes the eggs." The man didn't sound as upbeat as Angela. If I were really selling the eggs, I'd take her deal hands down only because this guy was crabby. "What? He's coming back with another offer?"

"I can't seem to get into my computer and read my notes about your last conversation with Fred. Can you give me a rundown of your conversation?" I asked.

"Sure. Your boss only wants to split the number of eggs the Ayam Cemani lays. That's not how my people like to have the eggs. They are sacred and not to be split up. When I began to ask him questions about the size of the eggs and the color, he didn't seem to know what I was talking about." The man hesitated. "Listen, lady. I don't have time to chase fake eggs. Either he can answer my questions or not."

"Great. Thanks for your time." I hung up the phone and texted Patrick, again.

Obviously Fred saw how much the eggs could sell for, the IRS was nipping on his heels and he didn't have six months to wait for another batch of eggs from Bertie to lay. He was running out of time. Poor Jean. My heart felt so sorry for her. Then it hit me. Immediately I dialed Patrick.

"Hey, I'm just pulling up to TJ's house," he answered.

"Listen, I have to know everything about you. Why'd you stopped being a cop? What has happened to Jean isn't going to happen to me when I'm their age." I gulped back the tears.

"Roxy, where is this coming from?" There was concern in his voice. "I love you."

"Fred loved Jean too. He kept his IRS debt from her. Now her home, the only home she knows is about to be pulled out from under her. He was someone she didn't know." The tears fell down my face. I reached over for one of the muffins that just had come out of the oven and started to stuff my face. "I honestly can't live like that."

"I completely understand," he tried to comfort me. "I can come by tonight and I'll let you ask me anything and I'll tell you anything that I think you need to know."

"Now I feel stupid for getting so upset." I wiped the tear from my face and ate the rest of the muffin. "It's only because I've talked to those markets Fred was trying so desperately to sell eggs to without Jean knowing and all of the sudden I put myself in her shoes."

"I stopped being a cop because there was a drowning of a child from one of the summer citizens. It bothered me that I couldn't save her. It was then that I realized I wasn't happy. Construction comes naturally to me. Could you imagine ever going back to being a fulltime lawyer?" he asked.

"No." I wished he were in front of me so I could hug him. "Thank you for telling me about the drowning. I know it had to be hard for you."

"I love you. I'm an open book for you. I'm actually surprised that you didn't go sleuthing into why I had quit." He laughed. "But I think you leave your skills to find killers."

I laughed. "Go talk to TJ. I'm heading to the bank to talk to Emily's father who is the loan officer there."

"That's a gift in the hand," he noted.

"Yes it is. I can't wait to see what he says about Fred." We gave each other our "I love yous" and hung up.

"Are you sure you got it all under control?" I asked Bunny.

"I always do and now that Emily is here to help, I'm gonna feel a lot safer with that murderer on the loose," Bunny said. "I'd heard that someone had broken into Pet Palace while you were there. I'm glad you're okay, but you're not a lawyer anymore. Now the killer is after you for snooping."

"I'm not snooping." Her words caused me to think about my activities over the past couple of days. "I've just been at the wrong places at the wrong times."

No matter how much I tried to forget her words, I found myself looking over my shoulder throughout the day.

CHAPTER SEVENTEEN

The warm summer weather really did bring out people. Most of the year-round citizens drove their bikes since Honey Springs was a small town. It was unusual for me to drive my car and it took me a minute to find a good parking space that was central to not only Honey Springs National Bank, but also the courthouse where I needed to check on the status of my licenses as well as the real estate office.

Central Park was located in the middle of downtown. The sidewalk around it and different sidewalks leading to the middle of the park where a big white gazebo was, were full of people standing and talking. Even the dogs on leashes seemed to be having a good time.

The flags Mom had hung on the dowel rods from carriage lights were so pretty dotting all of the downtown sidewalks. The spring daffodils that had popped out of the soil around the park in the spring were now replaced with marigold, daisies, lilies, and a few wildflower beds. The Garden Committee had always taken great care of the land-scape in and around Honey Springs.

The courthouse was the tallest building and was located in the middle of Main Street. No matter where you stood on the courthouse lawn, the views of Central Park were amazing.

The medical building where the dentist, optometrist, podiatrist, and good old-fashioned medical doctors were just a block over from the courthouse and beyond that was Honey Springs National Bank. A couple of blocks on the other side was where Doris Blankenship had her real estate office and two blocks behind Main Street was a neighborhood where most of the people who worked in town lived. Aunt Maxi's house (the one she said she'd sell to Mom) was in that area.

If I had time, I'd walk over there to see if they were still there checking out the house.

The Honey Springs National Bank was a typical bank. The old concrete floor played a huge role in the ability of your voice to echo and bounce off the walls. When I came in the door, everyone stopped to stare. There were two large glass offices on the right and a teller line straight ahead. One of the doors had a sign that said loan office. There was a balding man sitting behind the desk. When we made eye contact, I offered a friendly smile and held up a to-go cup of Mom's lavender coffee, which was our biggest seller at the moment, and a couple of my apple honey crisps in a bag in the other hand.

"Can I help you?" the man asked.

"Hi, I'm Roxanne Bloom." I held the cup and bag out to him. "My friends call me Roxy. Are you Emily's dad?"

"Yes. Evan Rich." He nodded and his eyes popped open like he knew who I was. "Thank you for giving her a fulltime job this summer. I hope she was on time for her first day."

It was still noticeable that everyone was looking at us, and thanks to the echo, they were listening to our conversation.

"Yes. She's amazing." I pointed into his office. "Can we go into your office?"

"Sure." He stepped aside and let me go first. He closed the door behind us. "Thank you for the treats. I smell why Emily likes it there so much."

"Oh I don't think it's the smell as much as her talent in the kitchen." It was my opening to talk to him about Emily and about the plans she has for her life. "She's a wonderful baker. In fact, that apple honey crisp was made by her."

He took it out of the bag and looked at it before he took a bite.

"I'm here to talk to you about a couple of things." I was talking off the cuff but the more I thought about it, the more it made sense. "I'm not a baker. I'm a coffee barista. I opened The Bean Hive because of the need for Honey Springs to have a specialty coffeehouse."

Evan finished off the pastry and took a drink of the coffee.

"I know that Emily had mentioned to you and your wife that she'd like to skip college to go to some sort of baking school, and I have many contacts that I met while going to barista school." He intently looked at me without giving any sort of inkling he was buying what I was selling. "Listen," I eased up on the edge of the chair. I placed my forearm on the desk and leaned on it. "If she goes to college, it will be a waste of money. Trust me." I rolled my eyes. "My mother wanted me to be a lawyer so bad. I did that and went into debt, which as you know isn't a good thing." I gestured between us. "Especially since our mutual friend, Fred Hill, was in a bit of a pickle with the IRS."

His face relaxed and he blankly looked at me.

"But back to Emily." I pushed myself off of his desk and sat back in the chair. "I just want you to think about her. Yes. I made great money as a lawyer but I wasn't happy. I make good money as a barista and am super happy. Trust me, I know we need money to live on and Emily really doesn't understand all the financials of life like me and you, but there is something to be said about how being happy and working go together well."

"What is it you're not exactly beating around the bush about?" He cocked a brow.

"I'd like to mentor Emily for at least a year." I had no idea where this was coming from, but it seemed like a good idea. "I'd like to make her a temporary partner at The Bean Hive where she can get a real sense of what it's like to run a bakery, be the baker and the boss. I suggest she do all the things an entrepreneur has to do to make it a successful business."

His eyes narrowed. His jaw jutted backward and forward like he noodling my proposal.

"If she starts right now, at her age, she'll be so successful and happy." My head nodded to the empty sack that had her version of the apple honey crisp in it. My brows lifted as I waited for his answer.

"I could help her with a business loan and show her how to do quarterly taxes." Evan was processing what I was saying and I could tell he was liking the idea. "We can even do an LLC."

"You don't need to worry about a loan." The last thing I wanted for Emily was to go into debt at such a young age. "I've got the kitchen space and all the ingredients she needs to get through the first few weeks. She can use any of the money she makes to purchase items she might need," I hesitated, "like fruit." I sucked in a deep breath. "Not that I'm sure where we're going to get fresh fruit since. . .," I looked down for a dramatic effect and then slowly looked up at him, "Fred."

My lips thinned in a flat smile.

"He said that he was coming in here to talk to you about the IRS and possibly take out a second mortgage. Is that right?" I asked.

"I'm not sure why you know about my meeting with Mr. Hill, but if you think his business here at Honey Springs National Bank had anything to do with his death, you can forget that. We are a very reputable establishment." His voice had turned very stiff and rigid.

"Oh no. I'm not accusing anyone of anything. I'm friends with the Hills. Jean is very distraught and I'm also representing Louise Carlton and since," I tilted my head back and forth, ear to shoulder, a couple of times, "she is the prime suspect," I lied, "I'm trying to get down to the bottom of things. As well as help Jean get Fred's estate settled."

Now, I knew better than anyone that technically he couldn't tell me a thing. I wasn't executor of Fred's estate, nor was I their lawyer. I made sure I never really said that, if it was to try to come back and bite me. I had chosen my words very carefully so I couldn't get in trouble legally or professionally. These days, law licenses were revoked for the simplest of things.

"Well." He leaned in over his desk. His eyes darted around the glass walls and finally fixed upon mine. "I'll tell you one thing. That IRS thing, I think it's a scandal. One of them internet schemes and I told him too. He said that they even called him to send a cashier's check right away. I told him not to do that and that he needed to talk to a lawyer."

"A lawyer?" I gulped and remembered Fred asking me if I was still a lawyer when he came to Pet Palace with Bertie.

"Another thing. When I went to pull the property valuation, there was a pending investigation on it. At first I thought it was because the courts hadn't put the ruling in from the lawsuit with TJ Holmes. TJ came in here on Tuesday morning to withdraw a lot of money." His lips pursed. "I asked him about the lawsuit because I wanted to try and get Fred's paperwork. He said that the Honey Springs judge had them settle because Fred's been farming the property all these years. TJ's not satisfied with it. He said he got him a big city lawyer from up north and he was on his way to see him with the retainer fee."

"Tuesday morning?" I asked.

"Yep," he confirmed.

"Do you know what time?" I asked.

Evan used the palm of his hands and pushed himself backward. The chair rolled to the desktop computer behind him. He typed away and then pointed to the screen.

"See here. The timestamp for the teller was ten a.m." He pointed to the screen.

"May I?" I asked before I got up, assuming he wanted me to walk over.

"Absolutely." He motioned for me. "Do you think TJ could've killed him?" He looked over his shoulder.

"No, because you just gave him an alibi." I wondered why he'd wanted Spencer to think he was at the marina doing work for Big Bib.

"I'm only letting you see this because you're not only giving my daughter a shot, but I like Louise and my other daughter really likes Tank." He smiled.

"Thank you, I do think Emily is going to surprise you." Thinking of

Tank automatically made me smile. "As for Tank. Your family is a perfect fit." I took a step back and thanked Evan for his time.

On my way out of the bank, I called Spencer to fill him in on what I'd found out. Even though I knew he was going to be mad that I'd decided to look into it.

"Don't get mad when I tell you this," I said when I raced down the street toward the courthouse. "But TJ Holmes lied to you about where he was the morning Fred was murdered."

"And you know this why?" Spencer asked on the other end of the phone.

"First off, Patrick and I went out on his boat and I just so happened to see Big Bib—"

"Just so happened, did you?" he interrupted me. There wasn't happiness in his voice. "Go on. I'm listening."

"According to Big Bib, TJ told him to confirm that he was there when he wasn't. But he does have an alibi, so he didn't kill Fred." I stopped talking to greet the silence from the other end of the phone. I continued, "TJ didn't like the verdict from the judge about the whole property survey, so he's decided to get a fancy lawyer from the city. The lawyer required a retainer. TJ came to the bank around the time you said Fred was attacked. I'm sure if you check out the law firm he hired, you'd find out he has an alibi."

"You think?" he asked sarcastically.

"I'm sorry, but people tell me things." I laughed. "So here's what we know."

The sun was so bright; I nearly knocked into someone when I was going up the steps of the courthouse.

"Sorry," I apologized to the person I almost took out.

"Don't be sorry." Spencer thought I was talking to him and I let him go with it. "I wonder why he lied."

"Maybe he thought if he told you that he wasn't happy with the verdict and was seeking a new lawsuit, it gave him a motive because I also found out that Fred owed the IRS a large amount of back taxes." I looked down the hall for the clerk's office.

Ida Combs was standing next to a filing cabinet. Her hair was still up in the bun, but she had on a different pair of cat-eye glasses.

"I'll head out to see him." When he said that, my *oh no* meter went off because Patrick was going to head over there.

"Maybe you should go by the bank first and get a printout of TJ's bank statement from Evan Rich so it shows he has an alibi and proved he lied, so you can ask him why he lied." It was such a good response and also gave me time to get Patrick out of TJ's house.

"Why don't you keep the hot coffee coming while I do my job." The stress in his voice made me pause.

"I'm sorry. I overstepped my bounds. But at least I know Louise didn't do it." I just had to throw that in.

"I'll let you go." Spencer had his fill of me.

"Wait," I stopped him from hanging up on me. "Is Hill's Orchard still closed? Because I need to buy his apples."

"No. It's going to be closed until I can bring this investigation to a close." There didn't seem to be any swaying him.

"But I can just go to one of the apple trees in the way back and pick my own apples. Not near the crime scene." I thought I'd give it a shot.

"No. Final answer is no. You're just going to have to go to the Farmer's Market and get someone else's apples." Again, his words were strong and not wavering.

"Those farmers aren't from here. I'm sure Jean could use the extra money, not to mention it's for Low-retta Bebe and the Southern Women's Club summer lunch." I knew he'd know how urgent it was if I threw in Loretta's name.

He did laugh at my pronunciation of her name, but it still wasn't enough to sway him.

"It looks like you're going to have to come up with a different idea." He sighed. "I've got to go." He clicked off before I could protest one more time.

"Can I help you?" Ida slipped her glasses off of her face.

"Umm." I clicked on Patrick's name. "I'm looking to see if my license is here." I hit the keyboard to text Patrick to get out of TJ's house because Spencer was on his way over there. I slipped the phone back into my back pocket.

"The driver's license is two doors down." She pointed.

"Oh, I mean my law license." I looked up.

"You'd get the notice in the mail. We don't file those here." She gave me a sideways look. "Aren't you the coffeehouse girl?"

"I am. I was at Crooked Cat the other day when you were having your book club." For a quick second I thought about asking for the public records of the lawsuit between TJ and Fred but it seemed moot at this point.

"You really should join our book club. Leslie told us how you used to spend your summers in the bookstore with her mother." Ida's smile took over her face. "We could use some new members and since you're so close."

"Yeah. That sounds great. Stop by the coffeehouse this week and let me know the book selection. I've got a free treat for you," I thanked her.

The entire time I was talking to her, my phone was vibrating in my back pants pocket. Patrick had called and so had Jeremy. I called Patrick back on my way out of the courthouse and headed down the block to the real estate office. I still wanted to talk to Doris Blankenship about going to see Jean and what her true intentions were.

"Thanks for the heads up. Only one problem," Patrick seemed irritated. "TJ said he didn't call for a repair but since I was there he wanted me to look at getting electric to Fred's property line from his barn because he said that soon he was going to get his land back."

"Really?" My mind twirled with confusion.

"Yeah. He said that with Fred dead, he was going to open an orchard and needed electric to put in a sprinkler system too. He said he was tired of working on boats. I got your text a little while after I was looking around. Spencer did show up. He asked what I was doing there and TJ told him I was there to look into installing some electric work using Cane Contractors." He laughed. "He sure can think on his feet."

"He's a fast talker. But that doesn't make him a killer. I want you to look into that IRS thing a little deeper. Evan Rich said that Fred asked him to look into it because he was trying to get a loan to pay it off. Evan said they've not uncovered much, but it looks like one of those scams to him." I pulled the phone away from my ear when I noticed Jeremy was calling in. "Listen, I'm going to see Doris. Jeremy has been trying to call me, so I'm going to go."

"Love you." Patrick's voice was heaven to my ears.

"I love you too." I clicked over. "Hey, Jeremy. What's up?"

"I'm not sure what's going on with Louise, but she's called in again. I've got class tonight and I really could use your help again." There was a concern in his voice. "You know I wouldn't if I didn't need you. I could call the other volunteers, but you can do so many things and most of them can't."

When Aunt Maxi volunteered, she was in charge of doing the laundry and putting fresh beds into the kennels, not cleaning the poop and pee or filling up the kibble.

"Did you try calling Louise?" I asked.

"Yes. She said that she was just too upset to come in. I don't know. Something is going on with her," he was upset. "I can't miss class."

"It's okay. I've got some new help at the coffeehouse. I'll be there around five. Is that okay?" I asked when I looked down at my watch and realized it was almost noon. I had to get back to The Bean Hive and get Loretta's pastries ready.

One problem. I didn't have any fresh apples and Spencer wasn't about to let any produce leave Hill's Orchard until the investigation was over. I was going to have to do some fast thinking and baking.

"You are a lifesaver, Roxy." There was some relief. "I don't know what's going on with Louise, but she's getting worse."

"I'll check on her," I said and reached for the handle of the real estate office door. "I've got to go. I'm heading into the real estate office to check out some leads on Fred's death."

"You crack me up. Maybe you need to open a private investigation service at The Bean Hive." He laughed.

"No thank you." I clicked off and stuck the phone back in my pocket.

Doris, who was talking to the receptionist, looked up when the bell above the door rang. The office was tastefully decorated with a sitting area and an area rug. There was a drink station along the wall and the coffee smelled burnt. No doubt it'd been sitting on the burner for a while.

"Roxy, how are you?" Doris strode toward me with an outstretched hand. "Looking to sell or buy? I know someone who'd love to have that cabin."

"No." I shook her hand. "I'm here to ask you about the ranch property you were talking to my mother about."

"That." She clasped her hands and drew her chin in the air. "I'm not sure what's going on with the ranch, but I do have some other properties to show her."

"Oh really? I was thinking it was Jean and Fred Hill's house because Jean said you'd stopped by and insisted on looking around. When Mom told me about the house, it sure sounded a lot like theirs. Funny," I rolled my eyes, lifted my hands and shrugged, "Jean doesn't have any plans on selling. Unless she doesn't know something that you do."

"What are you saying?" Doris's happy to sell me something demeanor plunged. Her face hardened.

"I'm saying that you knew Fred was in financial trouble because you have an in with the bank. I don't think it's Mr. Rich, but someone. You found out that Fred Hill was in trouble. Where were you the morning Fred was murdered?" I asked.

"Some nerve you got, Roxy." She glared.

"Roxanne," I corrected her. Only my friends call me Roxy. "Did you confront Fred about it?"

"I think it's time for you to leave." She pointed to the door, never denying what I was saying. "Call the cops," she told the receptionist.

"You don't need to call the cops. I'm leaving. Leave my mother alone. My aunt Maxi is selling her rental to my mom." I turned on the balls of my feet and left.

I stood on the porch of the real estate office and dragged my phone out of my pocket. I had to tell Spencer my suspicions of Doris, not that it made her the killer, but she had something up her sleeve and maybe he could get it out of her.

"Excuse me." A gentleman in a three-piece suit stood in front of me as I blocked his entrance into the real estate office.

"Oh, I'm sorry." I held my phone up. "What would we do without these silly things? But they seem to always get in the way." I moved over and let him pass. He wasn't entertained.

CHAPTER EIGHTEEN

I just couldn't leave well enough alone. The card Jean had on her pie cabinet from Doris was more than Doris making a social call to the new widow. Doris wasn't that nice. Doris was out to make money for Doris and if she was already willing to find out information on Fred's misfortunes and capitalize on it, she'd do anything to get it. But anything as in murder?

There wasn't a clear-cut answer for Jean. Did she know about the IRS? It wasn't something I'd asked her. There just seemed to be a line between being tacky and tactful. In any case, my niggling curiosity left me hankering to go visit Jean one more time and maybe score some apples Fred might've had lying around the kitchen.

Just like before, when I got to Hill's Orchard, the sign was still posted that it was closed until further notice and the police tape was up. There were a couple of cars with men in khakis and blue short-sleeved polos and badges strapped to their belts. They were talking among themselves when I pulled up and stopped when I got out. There was no sense in talking them into giving me apples.

"Twice in one week?" Jean greeted me at the door of the ranch house with a pitcher of lemonade in her hand. She gave a little whistle and waved the men over. She set the lemonade on a small table on the porch where she'd already put out glasses filled with ice.

"They've been here day in and day out." The smile had faltered. "Do you think they're ever going to find out who killed Fred?"

We walked inside. The cool air conditioning felt nice.

"Jean, I hope they do and that's sort of why I'm here." I gestured to sit at the table. She nodded and eased herself into a chair. "Remember when I asked you about Doris Blankenship stopping by?"

"Yes."

"I'm afraid it was more than a casual visit. Doris is obviously in the real estate business. When you told me about her wanting to look around when you aren't going to move, it didn't sit right with me." I watched her face to make sure she understood what I was saying and making myself very clear. "The more digging I did in Fred's laptop, the more things I found as to why Doris would want to look around."

"Oh dear." Her voice cracked. "Did it have to do with that IRS email?"

"You know about that?" My brows furrowed.

"Yes, honey. But Fred said he'd take care of it." She wore a look of concern. "Did he not?"

"I'm not sure. It seems that he went to the bank to check about getting a loan from Mr. Rich, but Mr. Rich thought the email was a scam as well. It just seemed like Fred was smarter than that."

"Honey, I told you that he loved that orchard so much that he spent his time in there day and night." She tapped her temple. "But me, I'm a different story. I did pay what they called quarterly taxes."

"You did?" This was the best news all day.

"Mmm-hmmmm." Her chin lifted up and then down. "My daddy owned a grocery store. I worked in the office and had to help my mama do taxes. My daddy would moan and groan after Mama would tell him what he owed." She smiled at the memory. "He'd say, where'm I gonna git all this money? And dance around in delight because he knew Mama had always kept a small kitty of money that paid the taxes."

Jean Hill was a smart cookie.

"You know all the Farmer's Market money?" With her hands planted on the table, she pushed herself up to stand. She walked over to the pie cabinet and opened one of the drawers. She took out an old Folgers can and came back to the table with it. "This here is my small kitty."

She pushed it across the table to me and I looked in. Money had filled the old can to the rim and all I could see were one-hundred-dollar bills wadded up.

"We made good money at the Farmer's Market." She smiled. "So when Fred was stressed out, we went to the doctor. That's when Fred told me about the IRS."

"What about Bertie? Why was he trying so hard to sell her eggs?" I asked.

She threw her head back and laughed.

"Fred's daddy raised chickens. He had one of them fancy birds and loved it so much. When Fred talked to Louise Carlton at the Farmer's Market a couple of weeks ago and she showed him a photo of the bird, he immediately knew what type of bird it was. Now," she shook her finger at me, "he had to have it and he knew that if we sold the eggs, we could fully fund the retirement account we have at the credit union up in the big city. Fred didn't like to put all his eggs, so to speak, in one basket."

"Fred was smart." I was so glad to hear that Jean knew about everything going on.

"That he was. And I knew when Doris came by that she was sizing my house up, but it's best to keep my mouth shut and let things play out. Let her think we are in hard times and eventually she'd find out the truth. The one thing that haunts me is the person who showed up here the night before Fred died." Her eyes and mouth dipped down. "I truly think that person is the one who killed Fred and maybe took Bertie. I told Fred not to call all the Asian places."

I guess I shouldn't have been so happy, but I was so glad Jean knew what was going on and Fred hadn't left her in the dark. Maybe there was hope for Patrick and me with not knowing exactly everything from the past ten years apart, but making a life and future together.

"Honey," Jean reached over and patted my hand. "Someone sent Fred those emails and got us real scared."

"But. . ." I gnawed on all the news reports about scams that reminded people not to click on the links in emails, but Fred's were personal. "Do you think . . ."

"Someone was trying to scam Fred, he caught on and they killed him for it?" she finished my own question. "Whoever took Bertie, killed Fred."

Slowly I nodded. In the pit of my stomach, I knew she was right, but who was it? There were a lot of questions to be answered.

CHAPTER NINETEEN

"*P*lease don't fire me on my first full day," was the first thing Emily said to me as soon as I'd walked into the door of The Bean Hive.

"Oh no. What?" I was almost scared to ask. There wasn't much time before I headed to volunteer at Pet Palace. That time had to be spent making the pastries for the Southern Women's Club.

"Loretta came in," Emily's voice shook.

"She's scary." I was a little more relieved this was about Loretta, though I knew I wasn't going to be able to make the apple crisps the way I'd intended to.

"Beyond scary." Emily gulped. "She insisted on seeing the apple crisps for the Southern Women's Club Luncheon that she's picking up tomorrow. I looked at your order form hanging up on the clipboard in the kitchen and I saw you wanted to use Mr. Hill's apples. I guess you've not told her that you can't get the apples?"

"You didn't." I closed my eyes and when she didn't answer, I reopened them to find her slowly nodding, her brows and forehead wrinkled.

"She pitched a fit and took out of here lickety-split." Her eyes teared up. "It was awful. But that's not the end of it. She came back in and

123

swore me up and down. I told her that wasn't going to help nothing. But she just kept on."

Emily picked up a stick with some sort of food on the end of it.

"I was working on some new summer creations that are easy to grab and go. Don't get mad." She held the stick out to me.

I rolled the food on a stick around in my finger and thumb, taking a good look at it. Bringing it to my nose, I took a sniff.

"Waffle on a stick?" I asked.

"Chicken rolled in waffle on a stick." She smiled. "Take a bite."

Something about food on a stick made me extremely happy and sang to my soul. I was more than happy to take a bite. There was a crisp crunch that had a hint of maple syrup and then the taste of moist chicken entwined.

"Mmmm." The sound automatically came out of my mouth and got longer with each bite until there was nothing left on the stick. "Amazing."

"Right?" She smiled. "I offered one to Loretta and it made her stop cussing at me. Then," she took another swallow, "she started ranting and raving on how good they were and that she wanted to cancel the apple crisp order and have me make some of these. Maxine shoved her out of the way and they fought like two hens."

"Okay." I ran a hand down her arm to calm her. "Where is Bunny?" I asked.

"She headed on down to the Piggly Wiggly to get more fresh chicken." She gnawed on her bottom lip. "Are you mad?"

"Are you kidding?" I asked. "You're a lifesaver. I'm doing Jeremy a favor tonight and volunteering at Pet Palace. I've got so much on my plate with the murder."

"You're looking into Fred's murder?" she asked. "I mean, I'd heard you'd helped out with Alexis's murder, but not Fred's."

"I'm not necessarily helping, but let's just say that I'm making sure Louise Carlton is definitely not a suspect." I pointed to all the ingredients she had on the counter. "Do you have time to stay here tonight and make Loretta's order?" I asked over my shoulder on my way over to the freezer.

The last thing I wanted to do was to come back and cook all night long.

"I can," she called just as I walked inside and grabbed a couple of trays of muffins, donuts, and soufflés I'd already cooked for the next day.

"Then I'll tidy up here. Stick these in the refrigerator and get ready for the morning while you bake your waffles and chicken all night." I was glad to have her. "And when you talk to your parents, I think you'll be happy."

"Did you talk to my dad?" she asked as she mixed her ingredients.

"I did. I also told him that I'd like to mentor you for at least a year. During that time, I told him I'd like for you to do most, if not all, of the baking for The Bean Hive. You need to come up with a business model, tax ID, and I'd pay you like you were renting the space from me. All the sales you make from your goodies are yours. It's only fair."

I didn't have to ask her if she was happy. Her squeal and that she was jumping up and down told me she was beyond excited.

"Roxy, you are amazing." Her eyes teared. "Thank you."

We gave each other a quick hug because the sound of voices came from the coffeehouse. I left Emily in the kitchen and found a few customers at the register.

After I made them each an Americano and I made myself one, I walked over and sat down on one of the stools that overlooked the lake. There were so many things that weren't adding up.

Jean Hill knew everything about her husband and their business, which by ignorance I thought was just his. Literally, Jean stood in the background and was probably the brains of the business while Fred spent all his time in the fields making the crop as good as he could.

I watched as the boats zoomed up to the wake zone and geared down, barely putt-ing across the no wake zone.

I pulled my phone out of my pocket and dialed Louise. When she didn't answer, I left a message on her machine.

"Hi, Louise. It's Roxy. Listen," I tugged the phone closer to my mouth, "I know you've got an alibi for Fred's death. But I do have to question you about Bertie's eggs. Where are those eggs? Did you sell them?"

If she did sell them and told them that Fred had the bird, it was enough motive for someone to confront Fred and kill him. I couldn't help but think that Fred was taken off guard because he didn't seem to fight back; he was working on the orchard and not with Bertie. From what I understood, she was in her shed. Or was she?

"Hey, Jean." I quickly dialed her up. "Do you know if Bertie was in her shed after Fred had died?"

There was silence on the other end of the phone.

"I'm ashamed to admit that I don't know." Her voice quivered. "I'd gone to my sister's house. When I got back, Bertie was the last thing on my mind and when you stopped by, it was then that I remembered her. I knew he had enough feed in there for her for a lifetime."

"I wonder if the person took Bertie at the same time they killed Fred." I was thinking out loud.

"I'm not sure." She fell silent.

"I'm sorry to bug you. I just can't stop thinking this whole thing has to do with Bertie." I hung up the phone and knew it was time to call Spencer.

"It's me," I left on his voicemail, sure he didn't pick up because he was tired of me trying to investigate his case. "I went to see Jean and she knew all about the IRS emails. Apparently, she and Fred paid taxes, so I can't help but think someone was trying to scam him for money. Do you think the person who showed up in black was behind the emails? They came to collect on the IRS payment because they thought Fred was stupid or something. Then Fred shooed them off, so the next morning they came back and that's when they confronted Fred and took Bertie." I took a breath. "Because Jean has no idea if Bertie was taken when Fred was killed or not."

I pushed the end button and tucked my phone back into my pocket. My thoughts were more rambled than ever. TJ Holmes and Louise

Carlton had both motives and alibis, but where did Doris Blankenship fit in. I dragged the cup of Americano up to my lips and took a sip. When the bell over the coffeehouse door dinged, I got up off the stool and headed back toward the counter to wait on the customer.

"You." I rudely pointed to the man in the suit that I'd nearly knocked over at Doris's real estate office.

"You." He grinned. "You need to stop drinking coffee." His eyes drew down to my cup.

"It's hard when you're the owner. Let me get you a cup. It's the least I can do since I really did almost knock you over." I walked around the counter. "So you don't live in Honey Springs."

"No, ma'am, I don't. Here on business." He nodded. "How do you like having a coffeehouse here in Honey Springs?"

"I love it. What type of business?" I asked and poured him a cup of Mom's lavender coffee.

"I'm afraid to tell you." He took the coffee. "You might have a shotgun back there for all I know."

"Try me." I coaxed him and held up my coffee mug to give him a little cheers.

"I'm looking to buy land for tobacco crops. Contrary to popular belief, tobacco is still the biggest legal crop in Kentucky and with all the limestone and bluegrass here in Honey Springs, it'd be a premium spot." He took a sip of the coffee, his eyes still on mine.

"It's none of my business, but I'm sure Doris told you there wasn't any land for sale around here." At least I didn't know of any that Cane Contractors hadn't snapped up.

That was one thing I loved about Patrick's family company. They were in the business of preserving our small town and keeping the land exactly that. Land.

"According to our mutual friend, Doris Blankenship, she said there's some orchard about to come up for sale because of some sort of IRS back taxes not paid." His words were music to my ears.

"Did she?" I asked, lowering my eyes.

Now I could say Doris had what I called. . . motive.

CHAPTER TWENTY

Spencer hadn't called me back yet. He was probably busy following up on leads that I'd given him earlier and if that were the case, Doris Blankenship would be on his radar. Right now Louise was on my mind and if I'd had enough time to drive by her house and check on her before Jeremy had to go to his class at the community college, I would have.

"Let's go, Pepper." I opened the door.

Happily, Pepper jumped out of the car and took every opportunity to sniff and leave his mark on all the bushes along the walkway of Pet Palace. His little ears perked up when he saw Jeremy at the door. He ran to Jeremy, giving Jeremy all sorts of kisses.

"You got a good one." Jeremy gave Pepper a few more scratches behind the ear before he stood up.

"Are you talking to me or him?" I asked.

"Both." He laughed. "I'm not sure what's going on with Louise, but I do appreciate all you're doing for me. I've really got to get these classes finished and get my degree."

"I'm so proud of you for that. Even though I don't use the degree I went to college for, it did prepare me for dealing with customers and customer service. My mom always told me that jobs can be taken away in a heartbeat, but no one can take away my education."

"Your mom is smart." He nodded. "I heard she's in town."

"Not only in town, but I think Honey Springs has a new member of society. She's already joined the Beautification Committee. And she and Aunt Maxi just might have a relationship after all." It was so strange to say that out loud. Never in a million years would I have thought it.

"Anyway, I'm worried about Louise. Even though she has an alibi, do you know anything about the eggs and Bertie that Fred adopted?" I asked.

"That was a strange pick-up call and I'd gone with her in the van to get the birds." He put his hands in the pockets of his pants. "They shut down a poultry farm and called us to pick up the hens and chickens that'd survived. We took the van because from what we understood, there were so many of them." His jaw tensed. "It was awful. All the birds were sick and we couldn't save any of them. We found Bertie in the office area. Louise and I took her. She'd called Fred on our way home because she said that he'd showed her a photo of a bird his dad had when he was a kid."

"Then what?" I asked.

"Nothing. Fred came to get her. It was a week later that he came back raising all kinds of hell about eggs or something." Jeremy shrugged.

"Do they know who broke in here yet?" I asked about the other night I was here by myself.

"Nah. They don't know nothing. I bet you know more than them, just like last time."

"I did find out that Fred had an unannounced visitor the night before his death and we think that same person killed him and took Bertie," I said and patted my leg for Pepper to come out of the bushes.

"Someone took Bertie?" Jeremy's jaw dropped.

"Yeah. It's awful. I just hope she's okay because I always think about people using her for cock fighting or to keep selling her eggs to make a lot of money." I shrugged. "So where am I tonight?"

"I've already got the cats completed because I knew you'd already done that for me and you love being with the dogs. So don't go into the cat section." It was kind of him to remember. "If you don't mind feeding the dogs and taking them out again, that'd be great." He tugged on his backpack strap that was over his shoulder. "The other volunteers will be here to relieve you. If they aren't, call Louise."

"I've called her and left a message. She's not called me back." I wanted to let him know.

Pepper and I walked into Pet Palace but not before I locked and double locked the front door. Evidently, I wasn't careful enough the other night. Hopefully the intruder found out there was nothing there and I certainly didn't bring the laptop back.

"What did that laptop have on it that the intruder wanted?" I asked Pepper. He wagged his tail as if he was answering me. "You are so cute." I scratched his head and walked behind the counter to check the volunteer schedule to see when the next group would be in. It wasn't like someone was there all night, but Louise generally had two people come in around eleven to make sure everything was good and all the animals were ready for the night.

Aunt Maxi loved to volunteer but I didn't want her here when there'd been an intruder, which in my gut I knew was the killer.

The volunteers on the schedule had been crossed out over the past couple of days. My name was written into the time slots Jeremy had asked me to work. Had the volunteers decided not to come because of what had happened to me? Or was it the fact that they'd heard Louise was a suspect in the murder of Fred Hill, which we knew wasn't true. People were funny when they didn't want to be associated to a crime. Poor Louise. I didn't blame her for going into hiding while this got cleared up. But if she really wanted me to look into things, she really should be answering my calls.

I picked up the line and dialed her number in hopes she'd see it was Pet Palace on her caller ID and pick up. This was her life as well as her pride and joy. When her answering machine picked up, I left another quick message to call me about the case. I threw in there something about my license so it would freak her out to call me back.

"I know we don't have to see the cats," I said to Pepper, "but we need to make sure the back door is locked because I swear the intruder came in through an unlocked back door."

I flipped off the lights in the entrance area of Pet Palace. The last of the summer day sun was streaming its orange rays through the front doors and giving a little warmth to the air-conditioned room. Louise kept it nice and cool inside. She claimed that most of the animals had lived in such harsh conditions that she could at least provide them with comfortable nights. She did way more than that. If it weren't for her and Pet Palace, all of the animals would be out living on the streets or who knew where.

"Come on." I snapped toward Pepper who really wanted to go see the dogs. "Fine. You stay here."

When I got to the door that led to the cats, I opened it and the lights were still on. The cats stood at their kennels and meowed.

"Hey, guys." I looked into the first few kennels and noticed their litter boxes hadn't been changed and some of the water had hair floating in it. "This can't be right."

Jeremy did say that I only had to do the dogs because he'd done the cats.

"Oh well." I let out an exhausted sigh when I realized he'd told me wrong and meant the opposite. "It looks like you've got me tonight."

None of the litter boxes had been cleaned nor the water bowls refilled, I noticed when I walked down the kennels to the end where on the other side of the door Louise kept the litter bags, food, cat toys, extra blankets, beds and anything else they could possibly need.

I flipped on the light after I opened the door.

"Errr, errr, errr!" Bertie screamed from a car kennel that was sitting on the floor. The door to the outside was open and there stood Jeremy.

CHAPTER TWENTY-ONE

"*Y*ou just couldn't leave well enough alone, could you." Jeremy shoved me back into the first set of cat kennels.

I grabbed my elbow and winced at the pain.

"I'm not sure what you're talking about." My head swirled with what was happening. "Did you find Bertie?"

He grabbed me by the arm and jerked me closer to him.

"You know I didn't find Bertie." He dragged me down the hall.

"Where is Louise?" I asked when I remembered the volunteer list that'd been scribbled out.

"She's not going to be joining us anytime soon." His voice didn't quiver. "I didn't want to hurt you. I really didn't."

"Then why are you?" I asked. "I don't care about a dumb bird."

"No, but you care about Fred Hill and getting Louise off the hook. It was perfect. I should've known you were going to screw it up and get all nosy and involved. Why do women do that?" he asked and pushed open the door to the front of the building.

"I'd say it's in our DNA to wonder about. . ." I winced when he gripped the little fatty part on the underside of my arm closest to my armpit.

"Just shut up," he groaned. "I'm not good at this. None of this was supposed to happen. Fred, Louise, and now you."

He shoved me down into the chair behind the desk.

"Where is a pen when you need one?" he asked.

While he searched the desk, I reached into my back pocket to get my phone and dial 9-1-1. With one swipe of his hand, the phone skittered across the floor and landed underneath the filing cabinet.

"Really?" He smacked a piece of paper and a dull pencil in front of me on the desk. "Do you honestly think I was going to let you call someone?"

"Jeremy." I tried to talk in a calm voice, not the shaky voice that came out high pitched. "You really don't have to do this. I understand the money from the bird and the eggs is very appealing."

I was shooting in the dark, but if I was a betting woman, I'd put all my money on the idea that he'd found out the money he could make and it was all she wrote, meaning all over and done.

"You don't know nothing about life around here. You claim you do because you were a summer citizen, but growing up here and being poor was not fun. I've been working here for years. These animals live better than me and when I finally wanted an animal, Louise gives it to an old man that doesn't have much more life in him. He was old." Spit came out of Jeremy's mouth with each angry word.

"Take the bird. I won't tell. No one knows it's you. I didn't even know until I just saw you." Could I really talk him into just taking off? He did seem to stop and listen.

"You don't get it. I have to go to college. I can't afford it working here, but the animals need me. It was perfect. I could work here, Bertie would lay eggs every few months when tuition is due and I'd give the bird back. I went to Fred and told him I'd let him have her back in a few years. The old man wouldn't hear of it. He told me to get a real job to pay for college. Work hard. He claims people my age want things handed to them." He scoffed. "I've never had a dime handed to me. That old man was out of his mind and. . ."

His hand shook as he pushed the paper toward me.

"I even went to Louise and asked if I could go in on half the eggs if I found someone to buy them. Which I knew I could." His eyes darkened. His face hardened. "She said Pet Palace needed the extra money because winter was coming. Winter. Six months away." He shook his head.

He continued to mutter something under his breath. I danced the chair around to follow his every move. There was a shadow on the glass and suddenly Spencer's face was pressed up against it peering in at me. I tried not to stop looking at Jeremy as he continued to rant and rave, which I should've listened to so I could remember what he was saying, but I didn't. I barely motioned my finger for Spencer to go around the building because the cat kennel back door was still open.

"I understand." I agreed in hopes he'd just let me go and danced my chair back around as he stood in front of me. "Why don't you go on and take Bertie while I go clean the dog kennels. I'll just volunteer and that's it."

"You're working to get Louise off. I'm not stupid." He pointed to the paper. "Now write."

"Write what?" I asked and reached for the pencil.

If I'd not seen Spencer, I might've grabbed the pencil and took a swing at Jeremy but with the dull end, it probably wouldn't have made a mark.

"You have to say that you're leaving town with Bertie. You have to say something about the coffeehouse going under because it's a new business or something. God, I don't know." He nervously ran his hands through his hair.

"Hey you two." Spencer strolled in from the door of the cat kennel as if he were on a Sunday stroll. "What's going on up here? I was just driving by and I noticed the back door open. Since I did the same thing a few days ago, I've made a point to drive through."

"Thank God you are here." Jeremy pointed to me. "I just caught her trying to steal Louise's eggs and she had the bird with her."

"What?" My jaw dropped. "Do you really think you're going to get away with this?"

"It's okay, Jeremy. I've seen your bank records. There was a check that went through Honey Springs National Bank. I called the name on the check and they told me that you sold them some sort of very precious eggs that are sought after all across the Asian markets and it just so happens to be from the bird Fred Hill was murdered over. Bertie is it?"

"Don't come another step or I'll stab her." Jeremy jerked the pencil out of my hand and put it up to my neck.

"What are you going to do with a dull pencil? Give me lead poisoning?" I shoved hard on the floor with my toes and the chair went sailing back giving Spencer time to go for his gun and focus it on Jeremy while I got the heck out of the way. Within seconds the entire room was filled with officers and Jeremy was pinned on the floor by one of them.

"How did you know?" I asked Spencer when he walked over to give me a bottle of water.

"Everything that you were chasing was so in depth and most of the time when there is a crime like this, it's a little closer to home. I traced the records of Bertie and figured out the only two people who knew about Bertie outside of Fred were Louise and Jeremy. With a little investigation and checking into Jeremy's accounts at the bank when I went to check out your bank lead, I traced the large amount of money he'd just deposited into his account to an Asian market. It was there they told me about their deal with Jeremy for the next batch of eggs from Bertie in a few months." He smiled. "I'm glad you're okay."

"Me too." Patrick came in the front door of Pet Palace. "I think you're going to need to talk to Louise. She's in the hospital with dehydration. Jeremy had tied her up over the past twenty-four hours. That's when he took the eggs." He bent down in front of me. He ran his hand down my face. "I got your message about checking in on her and I found her slumped over. She told me all about Jeremy. I called Spencer and told him that you were volunteering and Jeremy was the killer. And I told him about the emails."

Spencer gestured for an officer to come over. "That's when I was at the bank and had to wait for the subpoena to be ordered to open up his bank records. That's when I saw the big deposit and got an image of the check. They told me about the eggs after calling."

"I was worried about my girl." Patrick cradled my face with his hands and kissed me. "I'm so thankful you're okay."

"I tried calling you so many times today." I looked around the room and realized Pepper wasn't there. "What about the emails?"

"I'd gotten back into the laptop and traced the IRS emails back to a server from the community college library. I went to the college and looked through the records of the students who'd swiped their ID card on those days." He lowered his voice, "Jeremy was there every single time Fred got an email. I used my old badge to budge my way into the bursar's office where I found out that Jeremy hadn't been paying his tuition and they were about to kick him out. Jeremy used the IRS scam to scare Fred into paying him payments. When he went to see Fred, I'm sure he told him he'd take the bird in exchange for the repayment. That's when Fred really figured out something was wrong."

"Jeremy did say that Fred said he was going to call the police in the morning. That's when he went back. He waited until he saw Fred come out of the house and disappear into the orchard. They exchanged more words and Jeremy had a knife on him, which is what he used to stab Fred. Then he grabbed Bertie." Spencer finished the rest of the story before he headed off to talk to a few more officers.

While Patrick took care of getting me a water bottle and checked on Pepper, I watched as Spencer instructed the men to haul Jeremy off. Sadness washed over me. Deep down I knew Jeremy was a good person and had let the money overtake his emotions and he couldn't see a way out of his financial situation. But it still didn't give him a good reason to have killed such a wonderful member of the Honey Springs community.

CHAPTER TWENTY-TWO

$\mathcal{T}$he crickets and bullfrogs were in a perfect harmony as the night started to take hold of Honey Springs. The cool summer breeze coming off Lake Honey Springs tickled my bare ankles; I brought my legs up into the Adirondack chair and tucked the blanket around my feet. I rested my head on the back of the chair and closed my eyes. Pepper and Sassy sat next to my chair as if they were keeping watch over me.

"Good evening," The side of the glass doors swept open and Patrick stepped out with two glasses of wine. He walked over and gave me a soft kiss before he handed me the full-bodied glass of red. "How was your day?"

"I didn't hear from you all day." I smelled the robust wine.

"I wanted you to rest." He bent down and rubbed the dogs with both hands. "Did you rest?"

"I didn't even wake up until noon." I couldn't even remember a time I'd slept that long, but when you're threatened to be killed by a dull pencil; I guess it took it out of me. "I called Emily and Bunny at the coffeehouse. They said they had everything under control. Emily did tell me that she'd talked to her parents. She'd like to work with me for a year and then decide if she wants to open a bakery. So for now, I'm hiring her to help me bake."

That was a good decision. I would be able to mentor her as she figured out her way. She was only eighteen and young. It was a long time ago, but I remembered how difficult it was at her age to decide what I wanted to do with the rest of my life. We know how that turned out.

"Tell me what you did all day." I wanted to hear about his day.

"I took Bertie to see Dr. Sawhorse." He referred to the local veterinarian. "He said she's only a couple of years old and has a lot of life left in her. I took her to Jean Hill."

"You did?" I sat up on my chair. "What did she say about Jeremy?"

"She was glad Spencer caught the killer. She was upset you were involved, and she hates that he's ruined his life." He shook his head. "I told her that TJ was going to sue her for part of the orchard, then she got a great idea. She wanted to know if he wanted Bertie since he did have some chickens and would know how to care for her and her eggs."

"Her lifetime alone would pay for the land." It was a brilliant idea. Jean was a smart woman.

"I called TJ to come to her house. He jumped at the chance. I gave him the names of the Asian markets Fred had been talking too. He didn't waste any time. He called one of the markets and already made a deal before he left Jean's." Patrick lifted his glass to his lips.

The silence was so welcomed. It helped get my mind back to thinking about the coffeehouse and how I couldn't wait to get back there in the morning.

"I also got Jean some employees. I told her I'd help her with her books and employees. She was happy to know that the orchard could stay open." He smiled. "She gave me a basket of apples to give you."

"Too late now. Loretta Bebe's order was already filled with chicken and waffles on a stick." The sound of it was ridiculous, but it was so tasty.

"On a stick?" Patrick's head tilted.

"New creation from Emily." It was going to be great to have her around. She had a creative mind.

"I also went to see Doris Blankenship to tell her to leave Jean alone. There wasn't going to be any sale of the orchard. And you aren't going to believe who was in her office," he said.

"Oh, gossip." I uncurled my feet and scooted back into the chair. "I could use some gossip."

"It's not gossip. Your mom has decided that she wants to be a real estate agent under Doris." His laugh echoed off the lake.

"What?" I asked in disbelief.

"Yup. She said that she loved looking around at houses the last few days and Doris was looking for someone to work with her since she's the only agent around here. With the summer citizens, Doris can't show everyone property. Your mom is studying away and is going to take the test to get her license." His face stilled. "Are you okay with her living here?"

"You know." I took another sip. "I'm okay. I'm more than okay."

"I want to talk to you about my last ten years." He paused. "Like I said about the cop thing. I'm not cut out to see the bad side of that profession. I can't deal with people dying and when you work near a lake community, people are going to drown. I just couldn't do it. The rest of the past ten years I've been working with the family company and thinking about you. I rarely dated and when I did, my heart was always with you. I knew you were married. I was willing to just live my life here in the home that still had your presence."

I pushed myself out of the chair. I took his wine and set both glasses on the deck floor before I sat down in his lap and let the moment take us away.

THE END

Keep reading for a sneak peek of the next book in the series. Freshly Ground Murder is now available to purchase on Amazon.

Oh…real quick before you keep scrolling. I've got a story for y'all. A real story.

Whooo hooo!! I'm so glad we are a week out from last Coffee Chat with Tonya and happy to report the poison ivy is almost gone! But y'all we got more issues than Time magazine up in our family.

When y'all ask me if my real life ever creeps into books, well…grab your coffee because here is a prime example!

My sweet mom's birthday was over the weekend. Now, I'd already decided me and Rowena was going to stay there for a couple of extra days.

On her birthday, Sunday, Tracy and David were there too, and we were talking about what else...poison ivy! I was telling them how I can't stand not shaving my legs. Mom and Tracy told me they don't shave daily and I might've curled my nose a smidgen. And apparently it didn't go unnoticed.

I went inside the house to start cooking breakfast for everyone and mom went up to her room to get her bathing suit on and Tracy was with me. All the men were already outside on the porch.

The awfulest crash came from upstairs and my sister tore out of that kitchen like a bat out of hell and I kept flipping the bacon. My mom had fallen...shaving her legs!

Great. Now it's my fault.

Her wrist was a little stiff but she kept saying she was fine. We had a great day. We celebrated her birthday, swam, and had cake. When it came time for everyone to leave but me and Ro, I told mom that she should probably go get an x-ray because her wrist was a little swollen.

After a lot of coaxing, she agreed and I put my shoes on and told Tracy, David, and Eddy to go on home and we'd call them.

My mama looked me square in the face and said, "You're going with that top knot on your head?"

I said, "yes."

She sat back down in the chair and said, "I'm not going with you lookin' like that."

"Are you serious?" I asked.

"Yes. I'm dead serious. I'm not going with you looking like that. What if we see someone?" She was serious, y'all!

She protested against my hair!

Now...this is exactly like the southern mama's I write about! I looked at Eddy and he was laughing. Tracy and David were laughing and I said, "I can't wait until I tell my coffee chat people about this."

As you can see in the above photo, the before and after photo.

Yep...we went and she broke her wrist! Can you believe that? We were a tad bit shocked, and I'll probably be staying a few extra days (which will give us even more to talk about over coffee next week).

Oh...we didn't see anyone we knew so I could've worn my top knot! As I'm writing this, you can bet your bottom dollar my hair is pulled up in my top knot!

Okay, so y'all might be asking why I'm putting this little story in the back of my book, well, that's a darn tootin' good question.

This is exactly what you can expect when you sign up for my newsletter. There's always something going on in my life that I have to chat with y'all about each Tuesday on Coffee Chat with Tonya. Go to Tonyakappes.com and click on subscribe in the upper right corner to join.

Chapter One of Book Three
Freshly Ground Murder

Aah...

"I love you my big dark, tall and delicious yummy goodness." Happily I sighed, and then breathed in deeply the aroma, letting the Christmas Harvest dark roast curl up around and in my nose.

I didn't care what anyone said. That first sip of coffee had a way of creeping into my soul and tapping into a joy that I couldn't explain. The view wasn't bad either. Especially since The Bean Hive coffee shop had the best location on the boardwalk and view of Lake Honey Springs. Even in the winter.

Pepper, my Schnauzer and trusted four-legged furry companion, stretched and whined.

"You're my favorite salt-and-pepper guy." I bent down to pat him with my free hand and he rolled over, belly up for a good scratch.

I wrapped my hands around the warm mug and smiled as the tree across the lake stood bare, so tall as they stretched up into darkness toward the sky. The light snoring sound of Pepper and the wafted smell of the Santa Kiss Cookies baking, kept me warm even though the moon helped keep the winter chill in the air at five-thirty a.m.

"Want to go potty before we get started?" I asked Pepper like he was going to answer me. He sort of does. His tail wagged and he bounced around.

The chime over the door dinged and he bounded out onto the boardwalk.

"Which way?" I asked giving him the choice of left or right because The Bean Hive was located right in the middle of the boardwalk so it didn't matter which end we headed toward to find the green space Pepper needed. "Right it is."

In the darkness of the early morning, the twinkling lights strung along the boardwalk by the beautification committee lit our way. The poinsettias were bright red and perfectly nestled into the hanging baskets from the dowel rods of the carriage lights that dotted our way along the wood planks. The little flags hung down from the potted Christmas plants with a big gold star. In the middle of the star it read Christmas In The Park Honey.

None of the shops along the board walk opened as early as The Bean Hive.

We passed the Queen of the Day Boutique, Buzz In-and-Out Diner, Odd Ink, Honey Comb Salon and Wild and Whimsy Antique store, which happened to be my second favorite shop on the boardwalk. Bev and Dan Teagarden always keep back little treasures they think I'd like. They were always spot on.

The Marina was located on the far end and off the boardwalk. Pepper did his business while I glanced over all the covered and winterized boats that had so much life a few short months ago. If I closed my eyes, I could hear the rumble of the engines echoing off the limestone walled around the lake during the summer season.

Off in the distance was Cocoon Hotel. It was the only hotel in our small Kentucky town. There were so many seasonal cabins to rent that Cocoon Hotel was normally not booked. But that didn't stop Camey Montgomery from ordering coffee and a sweet treat from me for her hospitality area.

"All done?" I bent down and patted Pepper when he bolted back up the steps from the grassy area. The whip of the wind chilled me to the bone. "We need to get you a sweater from Walk In The Bark."

He yipped. He knew that name really well. It was the pet store located on the far end of the other side of the boardwalk and a place Pepper got special treatment. Why wouldn't he? He's precious.

The oven timer was going off when we got back to the shop

Pepper and I walked through the swinging door that led into the kitchen portion of the coffeehouse. In the spring, it'd be a year ago that I'd opened the door to The Bean Hive. A coffeehouse was exactly what Honey Springs, Kentucky needed. No place better than the newly revitalized and renovated boardwalk.

Even though Lake Honey Springs brought in a lot of tourists for the summer, our Christmas Celebration wasn't one to miss. From what I heard...I've never been in Honey Springs for Christmas, but the excitement around it makes me feel like I have.

I didn't grow up in Honey Springs. My aunt Maxine Bloom lived here (she's my father's sister) and he'd bring me for long summers here. As my memory served me right, it felt like home. So naturally when I got my heart broken, I ran to Honey Springs. While I was looking for some of Aunt Maxi's southern home cooking for comfort food, she gave me a knock in the head.

"You're gonna put your boots on and get down and dirty. It's high time you hold your head high and follow your real dream. Now go on and put some lipstick on." Then she brought me here. The empty building and dilapidated boardwalk had both seen better days.

"Oh my, my." I opened the oven. My mouth instantly started to water just eyeing the Santa Kisses. "I've outdone myself." I rubbed my hands down my The Bean Hive apron and couldn't wait to get my hands on the kisses.

Long gone was the musty smell of the restaurant before me. The smell of coffee was now infused in every square inch.

"Just one." I looked down at Pepper who was eagerly waiting for something to eat.

While I waited for it to cool, I gave Pepper a scoop of kibble and grabbed one of the domed platters to put the Santa Kisses on. They were going right on top of the counter.

The round cookie had the perfect light browning. I closed my eyes and let the perfect combination of sugar, pumpkin, chocolate chips, and nutmeg melt in my mouth

"Do I smell Santa Kiss cookies?" I barely got my cookie swallowed before I heard my landlord come in the coffeehouse and quickly arranged the first batch of cookies on the platter.

"Aunt Maxi." I pushed the kitchen door with the platter in my hands and watched her face light up with delight.

"You've got a good nose." I set the platter on top of the counter and went over to help her out of her getup.

She looked like a bag lady dressed in an oversized coat, big scarf twisted around her neck and knit cap pulled down on her face. Her cross body purse was strapped across her body and she was busy stuffing her gloves in the front pocket. When she tugged the cap off of her head, my jaw dropped.

"*Silver bells,*" she sang and swayed back and forth. "*Silver bells. It's Christmas time in Honey Springs.*"

Pepper yipped and yapped. He acted as though he didn't recognize her.

"What?" She looked at me.

"Your hair is really silver." I couldn't stop staring, though I shouldn't be surprised, but this was the first time I'd ever seen her hair look even close to her age.

She raked her fingers in her hair, making it stand up even more before she tugged a big can of hairspray from her bag.

"This weather does nothing for my hair," she grumbled under her breath and threw her head down, spraying that sticky junk all over.

"Go to the bathroom." I snapped my fingers and pointed my finger toward the bathroom the customers used.

"Give your aunt a hug." She ignored my comment and held her arms wide open, the hairspray still in her grips.

"You're something else." I gave in and hugged her, then she gave my hair a few sprays letting out a big cackle. I fanned my hand in front of my face. "I've got to get my Christmas Harvest brewing to overtake that smell before someone walks in and thinks we are a hair salon."

"What can I help you with?" Aunt Maxi asked.

She was really good at pitching in wherever and did so without asking most days.

"You can refill all the tea bags at the tea station. Refill all the to-go cups as well as set up the Honey Springs mugs." I nodded toward the end of the counter where the tea bar was located.

There was a hot tea, cold tea self-serve counter. It offered a nice selection of gourmet teas and loose-leaf teas that could be made hot or cold. The cute antique teapots I'd gotten from Wild and Whimsy were perfect if a customer came in and wanted a pot of hot tea. I could fix it for them or they could fix their own to their taste and as many pots as they needed.

While she did that, I headed behind the counter and started to concoct my Christmas Harvest Blend in light, dark and decaffeinated. I took my Bean Hive grog blend as the base. It was more of a full-bodied coffee that was perfect with the cinnamon, nutmeg, ginger and vanilla bean that was added to create the perfect Christmas Harvest blend.

It'd been so popular over the past few weeks, I couldn't even keep in stock the mason jars I filled and wrapped a red grosgrain ribbon around for customers to purchase.

Aunt Maxi was finished in no time and had moved on to the coffee bar on the opposite end of the counter. She glanced over to see if the six thermoses were finished brewing so she could put them in place. The coffee bar was on the honor system, which meant there was a jar where customers could put their money in and get their own coffee. Sometimes the coffeehouse got busy and it was those times that customers came in and only wanted a cup of coffee. It was a perfect system for me anyways. But the creamer, sugar, sugar substitutes, honey, cinnamon, stirs, napkins and to-go cups needed to be refilled.

It only took a few minutes for me to blend the grog and add the ingredients to get the morning brew started. The smell of the cinnamon really did make it feel like Christmas.

"Are you going to the tree lighting tonight?" I asked Aunt Maxi while I got started on the Gingerbread Mischiefs to make for the furry friends that come into the coffeehouse with their owners.

"Of course. You're going to love it." She ran her hand along the piece of antique furniture I'd turned into the coffee bar.

I was actually proud of the entire coffeehouse. I'd taken and redone all of it by watching all sorts of DIY videos off YouTube. The walls were shiplap that I'd created from painted plywood. The counter was "L" shaped with a glass counter top with all the goodies stored below. Instead in investing in fancy industrial menus, I took big chalkboards and hung them to the wall and over the counter. The menus listed the weekly specials and all the fancy coffee drinks I made to order.

"I can't wait." I scooped some more kibble in Pepper's bowl before I pushed through the kitchen to get more cookies out and in the oven as well as start on the furry friends' treats. "Plus I'm going to get a tree from the lot and get this place all decorated. I've been driving by the lot and getting really excited with all the fun lights and decorations."

With the current cold temperatures and light snow, it was just way too cold for Pepper and me to ride the bicycle to the boardwalk or even into downtown. Everything in Honey Springs was just a hop and a skip away so having a car was more of a nuisance than a necessity.

On the way back from getting more Santa Kisses out of the oven and putting the trays in the cooling rack, I grabbed the cinnamon, ginger, flour and cloves from the dry ingredients shelf and the oil, molasses and water I needed from the wet ingredients shelf. The gingerbread man cookie cutter was a perfect choice for my furry friends' treats. A surefire hit.

"Brrr… it sure is cold out there." Bunny Bowowski, my only employee, waddled through the swinging door with her brown pocket book snug in the crook of her arm. She hung it on the coatrack along with her coat. She tied the apron around her neck and around her waist, over her housedress.

"It is cold and I love it. Cold weather makes for a lot of coffee-loving customers." I smiled and measured, mixed and blended the ingredients. "How are you this morning?"

"You know. This weather makes me all creaky." She ran her fingers along her grey chin-length bob. "Plus this Secret Santa thing is driving me nuts."

"It might be driving you crazy, but the beautification committee has really outdone themselves this holiday." I wanted her to know that I appreciated all the hard work she and the other women on the committee put in to decorate the town. "I absolutely love all the board-walk decorations."

"I just can't believe I let Mae Belle Donovan talk all these people into doing a Secret Santa exchange." She huffed and moseyed over to me. "What are you rolling out there? It smells so good."

"Gingerbread Mischiefs for our four-legged friends." I pushed the gingerbread man cookie cutter down into the dough and placed the cut figures on the parchment paper.

She got herself a cup of the Christmas Harvest coffee and took a sip with her eyes closed.

"Good, huh?" I smiled at her reaction. The reaction from her and my other customers were far different from the last customers I'd had as a lawyer.

"You've outdone yourself too." She eyed the cookies on the rack and took a couple before she headed back out the kitchen door.

While I got the cookies in the oven and set the timer for twenty-five minutes, I refilled my cup to join the two women already arguing over who knows what. Bunny and Aunt Maxi picked at each other, but that's all it was.

"What are you two fussing at now?" I asked with a tray of Rudolph Quiche that was perfectly named from the red bell peppers cooked throughout.

My specialty was the coffee and all the fixins, but I also offered a breakfast item that was usually a quiche, a lunch offering and I was closed for supper. The food items were offered the entire week along with the simple desserts and pastries I made. During the winter season, I was closed on Sunday's. That changed once the warmer weather hit because customers loved to gather before and after church. On Sunday I'd spend the day making the food items for the upcoming week as well as changing out the chalkboard menus, which made it easy to come in here in the morning and pull out anything I could freeze.

"I wanted to know what happened to her hair." Bunny's nose curled as she took the plates of quiche from me and began to place them in the glass cases.

Aunt Maxi was wiping down the few café tables that dotted the inside of the coffeehouse before she walked over and turned the open sign on the door.

"If it weren't for that whole Secret Santa thing, my hair would be red like the seasonal color," Aunt Maxi said over her shoulder. "Who is my Secret Santa?"

"I don't know. We didn't write down the pairings." Bunny leaned her hip on the counter and held the cup up to her nose. "It's awful funny that they gave you hair dye."

"Why?" Aunt Maxi glared.

The bell over the door dinged. Otis Peavler shuffled through the door. The cold air whipped in behind him, causing me to look at the fireplace. I'd yet to get around to lighting it this morning.

"Do you mind grabbing some of that wood for me, Otis?" I asked my shop neighbor. "I'll get your usual."

Otis was the owner of Odd Ink, the tattoo parlor next door to me. I wasn't sure how old he was but he had to be in his late seventies or early eighties. Most of the elderly women in town always fawned over him, but Juanita Lynn Anderson had laid claim to him a long time ago.

"Don't worry about the Coffee Chips." He referred to the signature cookies that were always in the coffeehouse. "I'll just have a large cup of the Christmas Harvest blend with a little room for some cream."

"Okay." I stopped and watched him for a second as he stacked the wood into the fireplace and used one of the prelit logs to start a spark.

It was odd for him not to get a batch of the cookies along with his coffee. He was a regular and he's never not gotten the treats.

"Can I interest you in anything else? On the house since you made my fire." I poured him a to-go cup and slid it across the counter.

"Nah. Doc Kels said I've got to cut back on my sweets. I got a diabetes diagnosis." He frowned. There was such a sadness in his eyes. "It's going to be strange not having my usual schedule," his voice trailed.

There seemed to be more meaning behind his sadness, but I wasn't going to pry. I'd leave that up to Aunt Maxi.

"You and Juanita haven't had a fuss have you?" Aunt Maxi cozied on up to Otis and put her hand on this forearm.

"Girl, you better watch yourself," Bunny quipped. "Juanita is like one of them ninja people when it comes to her man."

Otis's attitude took a little lift with the attention and big smile on his face.

"Ladies, ladies." He *tsked*. "I've only got eyes for my Juanita."

"Then why don't she support you and come to church?" Bunny Bowowski acted as the church police. In a small town like Honey Springs, everyone went to church. Most of the time it was more of a social gathering than anything else. "Or why don't y'all just get hitched?"

"Why don't you two stop being nosy?" I asked and winked at Otis. "I can dig up some really good sugar free recipes if you want."

"Nah. I'm good. Vegetables for me." He gave a nod and headed on out of the coffeehouse, but not without being nearly knocked over by Louise Carlton and a pet carrier.

"What was his problem?" Louise glanced out the coffeehouse windows and watched Otis hurry back to his shop.

"He must be in a hurry." I shrugged and walked around the counter to see what sweet animal she'd brought from Pet Palace.

Louise was the owner of Pet Palace, Honey Springs's version of an SPCA. Every week she brings a different animal to be featured at the coffeehouse to be adopted. It was a sticky situation with the health department, but we got around it and the community loved it.

Pepper ran over to sniff the carrier.

"This is Felix the cat." She put the carrier on the floor.

I bent down and looked at the scared kitten.

"What on earth did you do to your hair?" Louise focused her attention on Aunt Maxi while Pepper and I focused on Felix.

Felix gave a little open-mouthed hiss at Pepper when Pepper stuck his nose up to the carrier, but it didn't bother Pepper any. Pepper had stolen my heart when I went to Pet Palace so he was used to being with all sorts of animals.

"Well, Felix," I picked up the carrier and took it back by Pepper's doggie bed near the counter. "You're going to find a special someone and we are so glad to have you as our guest."

I set the carrier on the floor and opened the door. Pepper was so instinctive. He sat next to the carrier and didn't force himself on Felix.

"That darn Secret Santa." Aunt Maxi eyed Louise. "Are you my Secret Santa?"

"No. I certainly wouldn't've given you hair dye. And you certainly didn't have to use it." Louise shook her head and walked over to Felix. "He's a special fellow. He's been living in the woods as a feral. I finally caught him and it's taken a few weeks to get him to rehabilitate. He's very lovable after he gets over the initial shock."

She set a bag of kibble and some toys on the counter. It was just best to leave Felix alone and let him get used to the smells and sounds of the coffeehouse, which shouldn't take long since he's been in Pet Palace with all the noises there.

"I've got to run, but here are some flyers for the Christmas Pawrade." She took them out of her purse.

"Just lay them on the counter next to the cash register. That way we can give one to everyone who pays." It was going to be so much fun having a parade with all animals. Apparently, they'd been doing it for a couple of years and it's a perfect time for the animals to get a home for Christmas.

With the smooth Christmas music playing in the background, the warm smell of cinnamon floating around along with the coffee, and the flicker of the fire in the fireplace, my soul was full. It was already going to be the best Christmas ever. I could feel it.

Freshly Ground Murder is now available to purchase on Amazon.

RECIPES FROM THE BEAN HIVE

Velvet Chocolate Chip Cookies
Watermelon Pup-sicle
Southern Light Pound Cake
Twinkie Cake

Velvet Chocolate Chip Cookies

Soft-baked red velvet chocolate chip cookie recipe made from scratch. Plus, a bonus recipe for red velvet cake mix crinkle cookies below! This cookie dough must chill for at least 1 hour.

Ingredients

- 1 and 1/2 cups + 1 Tablespoon all-purpose flour
- 1/4 cup unsweetened natural cocoa powder
- 1 teaspoon baking soda
- 1/4 teaspoon salt
- 1/2 cup unsalted butter, softened to room temperature.
- 3/4 cup packed light brown sugar
- 1/4 cup granulated sugar
- 1 large egg, at room temperature[1]
- 1 Tablespoon milk
- 2 teaspoons vanilla extract
- 1 Tablespoon red food coloring
- 1 cup semi-sweet chocolate chips (plus a few extra for after baking)

Directions

1. Whisk the flour, cocoa powder, baking soda, and salt together in a large bowl. Set aside.
2. Using a handheld or stand mixer with a paddle attachment, beat the butter on high speed until creamy, about 1 minute. Scrape down the sides and the bottom of the bowl as needed. Beat in the brown sugar and granulated sugar until combined and creamy, about 1 minute. Beat in the egg, milk, and vanilla extract, scraping down the sides and bottom of the bowl as needed. Once mixed, add the food coloring and beat until combined. Turn the mixer off and pour the dry ingredients

into the wet ingredients. Turn the mixer on low and slowly beat until a very soft dough is formed. Beat in more food coloring if you'd like the dough to be brighter red. On low speed, beat in the chocolate chips. The dough will be sticky.

3. Cover the dough tightly with aluminum foil or plastic wrap and chill for at least 1 hour (and up to 3 days-- see make ahead tip). Chilling is mandatory.

4. Preheat oven to 350°F. Line two large baking sheets with parchment paper or silicone baking mats. Set aside.

5. Scoop 1.5 Tablespoons of dough and roll into a ball, as pictured above. Place 9 balls onto each baking sheet. Bake each batch for 10-11 minutes. The cookies may have only spread slightly, that's ok. Simply press down on the warm cookies to slightly flatten and form crinkles. Stick a few chocolate chips into the tops of the warm cookies.

6. Allow the cookies to cool on the cookie sheet for 5 minutes before transferring to a wire rack to cool completely.

Watermelon Pup-sicle

Pepper's favorite warm day treat.

Ingredients

- A quarter of a watermelon [[I opted for seedless]]
- One can of coconut milk

Directions

1. Scoop out about 1/4 of the melon or all of the melon if you aren't going to eat any.
2. Blend together with the can of coconut milk – add more watermelon if you want a darker pink.
3. Pour into ice cube tray and wait.

Southern Light Pound Cake

Ingredients

- 1 cup butter, softened
- 1 1/2 cups sugar
- 3 large eggs
- 2 cups all-purpose soft-wheat flour or you can substitute gluten free which I often do because Eddy is gluten free.
- 1/2 cup milk
- 1 teaspoon almond extract
- 1 teaspoon vanilla extract

Directions

1. Preheat oven to 300°. Beat butter at medium speed with a heavy-duty electric stand mixer until creamy. Gradually add sugar, beating 3 to 5 minutes or until light and fluffy. Add eggs, 1 at a time, beating just until yellow disappears.
2. Add flour to butter mixture alternately with milk, beginning and ending with flour. Beat at low speed just until blended after each addition. Stir in extracts. Pour into a lightly greased and floured 9-inch round cake pan.
3. Bake at 300° for 50 to 60 minutes or until a wooden pick inserted in center comes out clean. Cool in pan on a wire rack 10 minutes. Remove from pan to wire rack; cool completely (about 1 hour).

Twinkie Cake

Submitted by reader Robin Kyle

Ingredients

- Twinkie Layer Cake Ingredients:
- 1 box yellow cake mix (I used Duncan Hines)
- 5.1 oz box instant vanilla pudding (the large box)
- 1 cup water
- 1 stick salted butter, melted and cooled slightly
- 4 large eggs, lightly beaten

Filling/Frosting Ingredients

- 1 stick salted butter, slightly softened
- 1/4 cup heavy cream
- 1 tsp vanilla
- 7 oz jar marshmallow creme
- 3 1/2 cups powdered sugar
- Sprinkles

Directions

1. Preheat oven to 350
2. Butter and flour 2 (8 inch) round cake pans and set aside
3. In the bowl of your mixer, combine eggs and butter. Add water, pudding mix, and cake mix and beat on medium for about a minute, until batter is smooth and thick
4. Spread evenly in prepared pans and bake for about 20 -25 mins or until tops spring back when lightly touched, or a toothpick inserted in center of cake comes out clean

5. Cool cakes for a few minutes in the pans, then turn out on to wire racks to finish cooling

For frosting/filling

1. Beat butter and vanilla in your mixer until combined. Add marshmallow cream and beat until smooth. Slowly add powdered sugar until just combined. Add heavy cream, Increase speed to high, and beat for one minute, until light, smooth and fluffy.
2. Spread half of filling/frosting on bottom cake layer, then add the second cake layer on top of filling/frosting. Spread the other half of filling/frosting on the top layer of the cake. Add sprinkles on top
3. Chill for at least 30 minutes and serve.

If you enjoyed reading this book as much as I enjoyed writing it then be sure to return to the Amazon page and leave a review.

Go to Tonyakappes.com for a full reading order of my novels and while there join my newsletter. You can also find links to Facebook, Instagram and Goodreads.

Join like-minded readers like YOU in the Cozy Krew Facebook Group for dream casting, fan theories, and live Q & A's. It's like a BIG GIANT BOOK CLUB! But if you want to have your own book club, be sure you let me know! I love to send goodies.

Also By Tonya Kappes

A Camper and Criminals Cozy Mystery
BEACHES, BUNGALOWS, & BURGLARIES
DESERTS, DRIVERS, & DERELICTS
FORESTS, FISHING, & FORGERY
CHRISTMAS, CRIMINALS, & CAMPERS
MOTORHOMES, MAPS, & MURDER
CANYONS, CARAVANS, & CADAVERS
HITCHES, HIDEOUTS, & HOMICIDE
ASSAILANTS, ASPHALT, & ALIBIS
VALLEYS, VEHICLES & VICTIMS
SUNSETS, SABBATICAL, & SCANDAL
TENTS, TRAILS, & TURMOIL
KICKBACKS, KAYAKS, & KIDNAPPING
GEAR, GRILLS, & GUNS
EGGNOG, EXTORTION, & EVERGREENS
ROPES, RIDDLES, & ROBBERIES
PADDLERS, PROMISES, & POISON
INSECTS, IVY, & INVESTIGATIONS
OUTDOORS, OARS, & OATHS
WILDLIFE, WARRANTS, & WEAPONS
BLOSSOMS, BARBEQUE, & BLACKMAIL
LANTERNS, LAKES, & LARCENY
JACKETS, JACK-O-LANTERN, & JUSTICE
SANTA, SUNRISES, & SUSPICIONS
VISTAS, VICES, & VALENTINES
ADVENTURE, ABDUCTION, & ARREST
RANGERS, RV'S, & REVENGE
CAMPFIRES, COURAGE, & CONVICTS
TRAPPING, TURKEYS, & THANKSGIVING
GIFTS, GLAMPING, & GLOCKS

Kenni Lowry Mystery Series
FIXIN' TO DIE
SOUTHERN FRIED
AX TO GRIND
SIX FEET UNDER
DEAD AS A DOORNAIL
TANGLED UP IN TINSEL
DIGGIN' UP DIRT
BLOWIN' UP A MURDER

Killer Coffee Mystery Series
SCENE OF THE GRIND
MOCHA AND MURDER
FRESHLY GROUND MURDER
COLD BLOODED BREW
DECAFFEINATED SCANDAL
A KILLER LATTE
HOLIDAY ROAST MORTEM
DEAD TO THE LAST DROP
A CHARMING BLEND NOVELLA (CROSSOVER WITH MAGICAL
CURES MYSTERY)
FROTHY FOUL PLAY
SPOONFUL OF MURDER
BARISTA BUMP-OFF

Holiday Cozy Mystery
FOUR LEAF FELONY
MOTHER'S DAY MURDER
A HALLOWEEN HOMICIDE
CHOCOLATE BUNNY BETRAYAL
APRIL FOOL'S ALIBI
Father's Day MURDER
THANKSGIVING TREACHERY

SANTA CLAUSE SURPRISE
NEW YEAR NUISANCE

Mail Carrier Cozy Mystery
STAMPED OUT
ADDRESS FOR MURDER
ALL SHE WROTE
RETURN TO SENDER
FIRST CLASS KILLER
POST MORTEM
DEADLY DELIVERY
RED LETTER SLAY

Magical Cures Mystery Series
A CHARMING CRIME
A CHARMING CURE
A CHARMING POTION (novella)
A CHARMING WISH
A CHARMING SPELL
A CHARMING MAGIC
A CHARMING SECRET
A CHARMING CHRISTMAS (novella)
A CHARMING FATALITY
A CHARMING DEATH (novella)
A CHARMING GHOST
A CHARMING HEX
A CHARMING VOODOO
A CHARMING CORPSE
A CHARMING MISFORTUNE
A CHARMING BLEND (CROSSOVER WITH A KILLER COFFEE
COZY)
A CHARMING DECEPTION

A Southern Magical Bakery Cozy Mystery Serial
A SOUTHERN MAGICAL BAKERY

A Ghostly Southern Mystery Series
A GHOSTLY UNDERTAKING
A GHOSTLY GRAVE
A GHOSTLY DEMISE
A GHOSTLY MURDER
A GHOSTLY REUNION
A GHOSTLY MORTALITY
A GHOSTLY SECRET
A GHOSTLY SUSPECT

A Southern Cake Baker Series
(WRITTEN UNDER MAYEE BELL)
CAKE AND PUNISHMENT
BATTER OFF DEAD

Spies and Spells Mystery Series
SPIES AND SPELLS
BETTING OFF DEAD
GET WITCH or DIE TRYING

A Laurel London Mystery Series
CHECKERED CRIME
CHECKERED PAST
CHECKERED THIEF

A Divorced Diva Beading Mystery Series
A BEAD OF DOUBT SHORT STORY
STRUNG OUT TO DIE
CRIMPED TO DEATH

Olivia Davis Paranormal Mystery Series
SPLITSVILLE.COM
COLOR ME LOVE (novella)
COLOR ME A CRIME

About Tonya

Tonya has written over 100 novels, all of which have graced numerous bestseller lists, including the USA Today. *Best known for stories charged with emotion and humor and filled with flawed characters, her novels have garnered reader praise and glowing critical reviews. She lives with her husband and a very spoiled rescue cat named Ro. Tonya grew up in the small southern Kentucky town of Nicholasville. Now that her four boys are grown men, Tonya writes full-time in her camper she calls her SHAMPER (she-camper).*

Learn more about her be sure to check out her website tonyakappes.com. Find her on Facebook, Twitter, BookBub, and Instagram

Sign up to receive her newsletter, where you'll get free books, exclusive bonus content, and news of her releases and sales.

If you liked this book, please take a few minutes to leave a review now! Authors (Tonya included) really appreciate this, and it helps draw more readers to books they might like. Thanks!

Cover artist: Mariah Sinclair: The Cover Vault